Feeding Time…

"What are you?"

Kissy's face remained emotionless, almost passive. "I'm a feeder," she said, her unblinking eyes still fixed on Jeff's. "That is the only way I can describe what I am in terms you would understand. I do not know who made me or why, I just know that I am, and it is my nature to feed. We are not all that much different, your kind and mine. It is just that my kind is much older than you could ever imagine."

"We're nothing alike," Jeff said. "You feed on people. On men."

Kissy shrugged and the ghost of a smile came to her face. "I feed on men, I feed on women. It is all the same to me. But don't you see, that is where we are a lot alike. Men, women. It is all the same to you."

"I don't murder people."

Kissy laughed. "No, you don't do anything that dramatic. Your kind just takes women and turns them into unfeeling lumps of flesh. You take away their identity, their soul, and over time that eats up tiny bites out of their spirits until there's nothing left. I feed on flesh and you feed on the soul, and that, Mr. South, is much, much worse."

Jeff knew Kissy was right. And he knew he was next…

ART
&
BECOMING

DREW WILLIAMS

Demonic Clown Books
an imprint of
KHP Industries
www.khpindustries.com

ART AND BECOMING
by
Drew Williams

Demonic Clown Books
is an imprint of
KHP Industries
http://www.khpindustries.com

Art and Becoming Copyright © 2004 Drew Williams

ISBN: 0-9747680-6-5

Cover art by KHP Studios

10 9 8 7 6 5 4 3 2 1

ACKNOWLEDGEMENTS

There are a lot of people I need to thank whenever I'm lucky enough to get something in print. My wife, Cathi, and my kids, Robert and Elizabeth. My parents, Robert and Evelyn Williams. My old high school English teacher Mr. S, and the gang from Serra High who made it to the reunion: Pat Oates, Mac and Joell McSheey, Dave Chlystek, Yvette Hill, Patty Mansfield, Chuck and Lee Ann Come, Maria Brady, and, of course, Ed Brady who gets a mention in every book because a long time ago I promised him I would.

I also have to give a shout out to some great writers and professionals who, through their friendship, advice, and patience, have made the business of writing a lot more enjoyable and rewarding than I deserve: Steve Lukac, Weston Ochse, Chris, for the cosmos, Kealan Patrick Burke, Brian Keene, Mike and Mikey, Coop, Jon Merz, Jane Letty, Mike Roden, Brian Knight, and the spectre to my darkness, Joe Nassise.

Special thanks goes to Karen Koehler and the folks at Black Death Books who are allowing this little piece of art to become once again.

This book is dedicated to two former girlfriends who will remain nameless.

I would never have discovered Kissy without you.

INTRODUCTION

An artist takes raw materials and transforms them into something new.

That's a line from the tale you are about to read, and it couldn't be more true of the author who wrote it. He is an artist, plain and simple.

Writing is like any other form of art. It has its raw materials, its techniques and styles. A sculpture emerges from the transformation of stone and steel, a painting comes from the transformation of paint and canvas. A book has as its raw materials; letters, words, and phrases. The writer painstakingly assembles these together with attention to theme and tone, order and impact. He creates a world and populates it with characters. He works to show you these characters as living, breathing people, not just as constructions on a page. He pulls you into their lives; into their dreams and desires, their fears and hates. He strives to get you to identify with them emotionally, to understand them intimately, so that when the important conflicts arise in the course of the tale you feel their impact as if they were your own.

Unlike other genres, this can be particularly difficult when writing horror. The reader knows something unusual is going to happen; it is a horror novel, after all, isn't it? The writer is therefore under more scrutiny than normal. The reader is watching and waiting for the world to turn sideways. They know that at any moment, maybe this page, maybe the next, the writer is going to do something to make reality bend to his whim, to introduce some element that suddenly shows that things are not what they seem. A horror writer has to work extra hard to make this passage from reality to unreality as seamless as possible without the reader losing his empathy for what the characters are experiencing, without the loss of their willing disbelief. He has to make the reader care. Writer Gray Braunbeck sums this up nicely in a passage from his *Fear in a Handful of Dust*;

Horror is not merely creating unease or suspense, nor is it simply letting emotions both light and dark bleed all over the page or screen. It should convey the sense of genuine tragedy that hangs over all our lives; it should scare us, yes, of course, no arguments, but there has to be an element of genuine loss connected to that fear - be it loss of life, limb, sanity, or loved one. Of all forms of fiction, horror shouldn't be satisfied with simply engaging the emotions - it should strive to make people experience every joy, every shudder, every tear and triumph; it must force them to assume the role of the story's characters, whether they want to or not, and live their tragedy as if it were their own.

Living up to this goal takes talent.

The kind of talent that many modern horror writers would kill for.

Lucky for him, Drew Williams has it in spades.

Drew is a wordsmith. He cares about each and every word on the page, artfully crafting them to achieve just the right effect. He is a student of language, with a doctorate in literature. Even more importantly, he is a dedicated practitioner of the craft.

I met Drew several years ago at the beginning of both of our careers. I found him to be a man of similar tastes and philosophies and we quickly became friends. Our debut novels came out only a few short months apart and by then we were working together on a joint collection of short fiction, *Spectres and Darkness* that would be released the following year. Through my association with him, I have learned a tremendous amount about the art of writing. The suggestions and criticism he has offered of my work have made me a better writer. And, dare I say, a better artist.

The tale you are about to read is one typical of Drew's talent. He draws us into the world of the artist, teaching us about the need to create, about the desire to transform, and about what can happen when the created yearns with a hunger greater than that of the creator.

I'm sure you'll enjoy it as much as I did.

Though with Drew, you are never sure if you are just reading or reading and becoming...

Joe Nassise
President, HWA 2003-04
Phoenix, Arizona
February, 2004

ONE

The dead guy's name was Henry Wallace. He was five-foot-nine, weighed a hundred and seventy four pounds, had brown eyes, brown hair, and was an organ donor. Of course his vital statistics lost their relevancy at 12:09 in the morning, a few seconds after Henry wrapped his lips around the open end of a shotgun. His arms, too short to allow him to reach the trigger with the barrel in his mouth, Henry had ingeniously tied one end of a string around the trigger and the other end around the big toe of his right foot. That done, all it took was a three count and a thrust of his foot for the double-barreled gun to blow off three fourths of the back of Henry's head and splatter bloody chunks of gray matter and bone in a the shape of a question mark on the kitchen wall behind where Henry sat.

Officer Lance Jacobs glanced down at Henry's driver's license and frowned. In lieu of a suicide note, Henry had considerately placed his wallet, his keys, and his twenty-dollar Timex on the kitchen table in front of him, next to the remnants of his last meal, a pile of Slim Jim wrappers and a half empty can of Diet Sprite. "Not even forty," Jacobs muttered, uncomfortably aware of the closeness in his age to that of the deceased. Jacobs compared the unsmiling face to the lump of flesh that remained above Henry's neck. Same jaw, Lance thought. Everything else was pulp.

"Morning officer."

Jacobs stole a quick glance behind and grunted at a tall, thin man wearing white scrubs and holding a clipboard.

"Hey, Phil," he said, slipping the license back into Henry's wallet. "You got here quick."

Phil Luxor, the senior driver on the graveyard shift for the Allegheny County Morgue shrugged and pushed his fist into the loose pockets of his lab coat. "We were in the neighborhood," he said, casually glancing past Jacobs at the remains of Mr. Wallace. "Same old, same old. Huh, Lance?"

Jacobs looked at the bloodstained floor and the nearly headless corpse. "Yeah," he sighed. "Same old, same old."

TWO

Phil Luxor was well-versed in the business of corpse retrieval. By his own estimation, Phil had picked up over a thousand corpses during his career driving the twenty-year old ambulance that had been converted into a pickup rig which Phil christened the Bony Express. About a third of them, like Henry Wallace, were the bloody aftermaths of suicide or murder. Handling the dead didn't particularly bother Phil, nor did the sight of broken bones and loose entrails that ended up garnishing many of his pickups. Blood was just another part of the job, nothing to get worked up about.

The only thing that did get under Phil's skin was the waiting, and if the years of corpse retrieval had taught him anything, the more grisly the death, the longer the standing around time. Henry Wallace was proving to be no different. Another ten or fifteen minutes, Jacobs told him soon after his arrival. Then the cops would be through and the body would be ready for the Bony Express.

Phil popped a stick of gum into his mouth and glanced at his new partner, Jeff French, as he waited on the opposite side of the kitchen for the cops to clear out. Without exception, Phil's previous partners had been world-class losers. Some, like his first partner, Stu Fendler, were incapable of holding down any job that required the use of the cerebrum. In Stu's case, Phil quickly found out that the man couldn't master the intricacies of putting files in alphabetical order or using a toothbrush. Guys like Stu usually got bored within a few weeks and quit to pursue some other meaningless career. Or there were those like his last partner, Gail Yakota, who couldn't stomach the often-gruesome pickups. She had quit her third night on the job after she and Phil went to pick up the body of a man who had been electrocuted a week earlier. One look at the purpling lump of fried flesh that used to be a plumber named Izzy Stewart and Miss Yakota hurled chunks all over the corpse's bare feet.

Phil was pretty good at sizing up how long a driver was going to last within two or three shifts, but with Jeff French it was different. For one, Jeff definitely did not look like someone who would be working nights loading corpses into a broken down ambulance. Jeff looked like someone who should be on the cover of a magazine. He was tall, muscular, and had the kind of cool, wavy, black hair that Phil secretly always wished he had. More striking were Jeff's eyes, easily the deepest blue Phil had ever seen. And though Jeff didn't say much, Phil could tell that he was no dummy. Deep in those eyes, Phil could see a world of experience and weariness that belied the man's age. There was no doubt about it; Jeff French was not the typical loser Phil usually found riding shotgun with him in the Bony Express. He was different.

And that made Jeff French interesting.

"Pretty gruesome, huh?" Phil said, pointing to the corpse. Jeff nodded, his thin lips pursed in a slight frown. It was only Jeff's fourth week on the graveyard shift and, so far, this was about the worst pickup he and Phil had made.

The entire time he waited, Jeff didn't take his eyes off the body. Slumped over the way it was, it reminded Jeff of someone waiting in a dentist's chair, except, of course, that most of Henry's teeth were stuck in the drywall above the kitchen sink. "What do we do with all the brains and stuff on the walls?" Jeff asked.

"Blood we don't worry about. Solid matter, we got to

clean up."

Jeff turned to Phil and rolled his eyes. "How do we do that?"

Phil opened up the small, red toolbox he always took with him on calls and fished out a pair of tweezers and a thin silver spatula. He slipped them into the oversized pocket of his labcoat before extracting a clear plastic bag from the box. Snapping the lid shut, he flipped the baggie to Jeff. "You hold, I'll scoop."

Jeff nodded and looked at the gruesome mess in the kitchen. Mixed with the blood on the floor and walls, broken teeth and fragments of bone were visible like tiny pebbles peeking through a thin covering of mud. The more eye-catching examples of solid matter, however, were the hunks of brain and scalp that clung to the wall above the sink like globs of gray snot. Absently, Jeff began to twist the baggie around his fingers.

"You okay?" Phil asked.

"Yeah," Jeff said, then adding. "I'm getting used to it."

THREE

Considering the amount of Henry Wallace's brains that was no longer inside his skull, the cleanup went rather smoothly. First, Phil took a second, larger see-through bag from his toolbox and placed it over Henry's head in order to catch any loose bits of flesh and bone that might get dislodged as the body was transferred. Then, with one hand beneath Henry's ass cheeks and the other hooked under his armpits, Jeff and Phil gingerly lifted the corpse off the chair and onto the gurney. A thumb-sized glob of blood and brains freed itself during the transfer, but the bag caught it before it could add to the colorful mess. Once Henry was on the gurney, Jeff and Phil strapped his torso and legs to the table. After the body was secured, Phil knelt on the floor and started to pick up the bits of Henry's brains with his tweezers. Humming softly to himself, Phil plucked up anything that looked as if it was once housed inside Henry's head, gave it a quick sniff, and then flicked it into Jeff's baggie. Once Phil was satisfied that the floor was picked clean, he turned his attention to the wall. Using the spatula, Phil scraped up equal chunks of brain and drywall and deposited them into Jeff's baggie. There was only one time that Jeff thought he might lose it. That was when a particularly tacky chunk of gray matter flipped off Phil's spatula and struck Jeff in the cheek. Jeff jumped back and batted at his face as if a wasp was buzzing around his nose, but he quickly regained his composure after hearing Phil laugh.

"It's only brains." Phil said, picking the blob off the

floor. He pinched slightly with his thumb and forefinger causing a faint line of pink ooze to seep out. "It doesn't bite." Phil motioned for Jeff to hold out his baggie. "Just relax, we're almost done," he said, dropping the dime size bit of brain into the plastic bag.

Jeff looked down at the pulp, surprised that the sight of a half-pound of matted brain, scalp, and hair didn't make him want to puke. He imagined it looked the way a small animal that got turned inside out would, like some mouse that got stuck inside a microwave for too long. There was no doubt that holding a bag of brains in his hands proved strangely exciting for Jeff, but it wasn't a rush he wanted to repeat anytime soon.

Brushing his spatula across his thigh, Phil announced the job completed. "You see any more goop?"

Jeff's glance went from the baggie to Phil's pants where a fresh pink stain had appeared on his khakis. It looked like a smile.

"No," Jeff said, handing the bag to Phil. He didn't like the look of the stain on Phil's pants. It was too new, too fresh. "I think we're good to go."

Phil held the bag up to his face and eyed the contents. "Weird, isn't it?" he said, giving the bag a little shake. "These chunks in here used to be part of this guy's whole personality. All his memories, all his thoughts, they were all stored in these little pieces of brain. This is who he was," Phil said, shaking the bag again. "Not that cadaver over there. This is where the real person is." Phil stared a few moments at the bag of brains then fished a black pen from his lab coat and wrote the date and time on the baggie. "Ever wonder where thoughts go when there's no more brains to hold them?" he asked Jeff as he wrote.

"Nope," Jeff said dryly. He shook his gaze away from the stain on Phil's trousers and glanced at the gurney. A streak of red was seeping through the clean, white sheet that covered Henry's head. This stain looked like a frown.

"Never thought about it."

"They go out into the air," Phil said, snapping the cap on the pen and slipping it into his pocket. "Just like radio waves. They stay out there, just floating around. You can hear them too. You just have to have the right antenna to pick them up." Phil tossed the baggie onto Henry's chest. "I'm going to sign out with Lance. You want heads or tails?"

Without a word, Jeff walked to the end of the gurney where Henry Wallace's big toe peaked out of the sheet.

FOUR

After the body was loaded and the pair was on their way to the morgue, Jeff asked Phil what he had slipped into his lab coat pocket when the two were cleaning the brains off the kitchen wall. "What are you talking about?" Phil asked. He was in the passenger seat smoking a cigarette, his feet planted on the dash.

Jeff didn't take his eyes off the road. "When we first started scraping the crap off the wall, you bent down like you were tying your shoe and picked something off the floor and slipped into your pocket. What was it?"

Phil took a deep drag on his half smoked cigarette before flicking it out the window. A few seconds of silence followed before he exhaled. "You saw that, huh?" Shifting his ass so he could face Jeff, Phil stuck his hand into his left coat pocket and brought out a small piece of plastic. "Souvenir," he said.

Jeff glanced at the thing his partner held out to him. It was a blood-coated ball the size of a nickel. "What is it?"

Gripping the object between his thumb and forefinger, Phil moved it up to Jeff's face. "Hearing aid."

Jeff glanced down and saw what at first looked like a small ball was really cone shaped. Tiny pinholes dotted the larger of the two ends. "That's the kind that goes into the ear, right?"

Phil nodded and slipped the hearing aid back into his pocket. "Yup," he said. "Goes right into the ear canal. When old Henry blew his brains out, it went flying." Phil patted his pocket before resuming his previous position.

He lit another cigarette and stared at the passing streetlights. Two miles later Phil asked, "You gonna tell?"

Jeff shrugged and turned his attention back to the road. The thought hadn't crossed his mind. "As long as you're not doing weird shit to their bodies, I don't care what you do."

"Thanks," Phil said, again patting his pocket. "It's for my collection."

Jeff expected the man to elaborate, but he didn't.

The two drove the last three miles to the morgue in silence.

FIVE

The rest of the shift was relatively easy, only two pickups and both of them were at local retirement homes. No gore, no mess, just two old men who went to sleep and didn't wake up. Though he didn't say any more about the hearing aid, Jeff kept an eye on his partner during their remaining pickups. But either because Phil knew Jeff was watching him, or that the pair of dead seniors didn't prove interesting enough, Phil didn't pocket any more souvenirs. When the Graveyard Shift ended an hour before sun up, neither man had mentioned the hearing aid.

After they brought in their last delivery, Jeff signed out with Kenny Sessoms, one of the morgue supervisors who never seemed to have any work to do. Jeff and Phil usually signed out together, but by the time Jeff had changed his clothes and went to the supervisor's desk, Phil was already gone. "Your partner was in quite a hurry," Sessoms said, pushing his clipboard toward Jeff. "He didn't even change out of his uniform."

Jeff scribbled his name beneath Phil's, then marking the time, slid his timecard into the punch clock. All the while, Kenny was bitching about the uniform being morgue property and that Phil had better not try to steal it. "You guys think I don't see what goes on," Sessoms bitched. "But I do, and I'm not going to put up with it."

Jeff put his timecard back into its place on the wall and slid the clipboard back to Kenny. "See ya," he said, then turned and headed to the delivery entrance in the back of the building.

By the time Jeff left work at a little after five, a slight drizzle was blowing from the east, casting a gray pallor to the early morning light. Standing on the rear steps of the morgue, Jeff turned his face into the mist and closed his eyes. Unlike the smell of blood and death he had been breathing in all night, the rain smelled clean. Jeff stood like that for almost a minute before continuing down Pirl Street. His apartment was ten blocks to the west, an easy walk for the twenty-four year old ambulance driver. But per his custom, Jeff traveled only four blocks before stopping in front of The Strand, a 24-hour diner and bar hidden between a donut shop and a woman's hat factory. Jeff plucked a cigarette from the breast pocket of his work shirt and lit it before stepping into the diner.

Not quite 5:30 in the morning and already a dozen men were milling about the small diner. A few of them were chomping on grease burgers, but most were lined up at the long bar sucking down draft beer. Like Jeff, most of the guys were just getting off the late shift, though a few of the men were trying to catch a quick buzz before they went to work. The men who drank there every morning did so mainly because they had nowhere else to go. No one to go home to.

When Jeff entered the diner, nearly every head turned to watch him come in. Jeff scanned their hard faces and felt their gaze upon him. Though he had been coming to The Strand regularly since he began working at the morgue, the regulars still looked upon him with a vaguely concealed mixture of indifference and distrust. Jeff was not one of them.

The men returned to their beers as soon as Jeff slid his butt onto a stool at the end of the bar. The bartender, a slight woman with reddish-blonde hair and the hardened look of someone who had spent the better part of her life pouring liquor asked, "What'll it be, hon?"

"Budweiser," Jeff said. "And a shot of Jack."

The woman nodded and headed to the far end of the bar where she kept the whiskey. Jeff pulled two twenty-dollar bills out of his jeans and laid them on the bar. When the bartender came back, she offered a quick, appreciative smile toward the bills before putting the shot glass on top of them. "You want to run a tab, hon?"

Jeff nodded through a cloud of cigarette smoke.

The woman pulled a crumpled notepad from an invisible fold in her dirty apron and wrote 'shot and beer' on the top sheet. Before ripping the paper out of the pad and sticking it on top of the antique cash register with the other tabs, she asked Jeff if he wanted any food.

"Not today," Jeff said

"Sure thing, hon."

After the bartender left, Jeff poured half of the beer into an eight ounce glass then placed the glass directly in front of him. He took the beer bottle and put it to his left. Then he slid the shot glass with the bills still beneath it to his right. "Father, Son, and Holy Ghost," he said humorlessly. He rested his folded hands within the triangle of booze and wondered who the hell he was.

SIX

Phil Luxor lived in an expensive, open-loft that he bowlderized by erecting a series of plywood walls that turned the massive top floor of his apartment complex into a disjointed maze effect of small rooms. Phil didn't like open spaces; he liked things compartmentalized. Living area on the Westside of the apartment; sleeping area on the north. His studio faced the east, so he could feel the sun as he worked. Phil fancied himself one of the last great beatnik artists, but at thirty-one years old, he was too young to have been part of the beat generation.

However, that didn't deter Phil Luxor from enjoying the role of the bohemian artist. A product of affluence, he didn't have to work if he didn't want to; a trust fund set up by his grandparents kept him financially secure. His becoming an ambulance driver for the county morgue was done on a whim, an act of impulse that allowed him to discover the gift that had lain dormant within him for his entire life. Phil Luxor had an insatiable desire to experience all that life had to offer, and, he reasoned, death was one of its most interesting parts. He wasn't sure if he was motivated more by his artistic nature, or his profound sense of boredom, but when he saw the want ad in the newspaper for ambulance drivers at the morgue, "no experience required," Phil applied. Since he wasn't a convicted felon or had any blemishes on his driving record, and he was willing to work nights, he was hired on the spot.

He soon discovered that the work was simple, almost

mindless. He drove through the city streets at night and picked up dead people. Sometimes Phil would take them to the local hospital, most of the time, they were brought back to the county morgue where he would drop them off to one of the attendants who would sign off on his tally slip then give Phil the address for another pickup.

But after three months on the job, Phil started to get bored. Handling a steady stream of corpses hardly proved to be the inspiration he imagined it would be. During the first two weeks on the job he completed a trio of paintings he called the "Going, Going, Gone" set, but other than that, his artistic production was nil. Death just wasn't as interesting as he imagined it would be.

Then Phil met Grace Finster.

It wasn't a formal meeting. Grace was dead, murdered in her apartment. She had been dead two or three days before the police found her on the dining room floor with a kitchen knife sticking out of her throat. Following procedure, Phil and his then partner, an obese Iranian named Turok who smelled of sausage, waited until the police told them they could take the body. While waiting for the go-ahead, Phil was drawn to the collection of framed pictures atop the sideboard in the living room. Most of the photographs were of Grace and a chubby, middle-age man with a bald head and a sour expression whom Phil assumed was Grace's better half. There was also a silver bowl on the sideboard that held Grace's keys, some spare change and a thin pair of bifocal glasses. Though he knew better than to touch anything at a crime scene, Phil plucked the glasses out of the bowl and held them to his face. Peering through their thick lenses, Phil could barely make out the photographs in front of him. He was about to return the glasses to the bowl when Turok called out, telling him it was time to get the body.

Phil turned toward his partner, and without thinking, slipped the glasses into his pocket.

That night he found out that he could hear the dead.

SEVEN

"Hey, I know you. You drive the Bony Express."

Jeff's head nap-jerked up. The blurry image of his own face stared vacant-eyed back at him from the dirty mirror that hung the length of the bar. An empty shot glass and a half-filled bottle of Budweiser sat inches from his fingertips. Jeff squinted and strained to get a better look at the face staring at him, his own face.

No, a woman's face. A flat mound of smooth flesh beneath a mane of auburn hair. No eyes, no ears, no mouth. But she was screaming, a burning switchblade of a scream jabbing through his eyeballs into his brain. She had no eyes but she saw. She had no...

"You drive the 10:00 to 5:00 with Phil Luxor, dontcha?"

Jeff swiveled on his wobbly seat coming face to face with a skinny, pockmarked man with a greasy, blonde mullet who hardly looked old enough to be in a bar. "You know me?" Jeff asked, his fingers instinctively stretching for his warming bottle of beer.

"Yeah, you're the new guy at the morgue, aren't you?" The pimply-faced man swung a long skinny leg over the stool next to Jeff and sank his rear-end onto it. Seeing the pack of smokes in front of Jeff, the man reached into his left jacket pocket and pulled out a lighter. "I got flame," he said. "But ran out of sticks. You mind?"

Jeff shook his head. "No, help yourself."

Needing no further encouragement, the man snatched the pack of cigarettes off the bar and tapped one free. He plucked it out with his teeth, and then made an elaborate show of flicking open his Zippo and lighting the smoke. As the man sucked in his first lungfull, the bartender took the opportunity to ask him what he wanted. "Rock-n-Rye," he said, blowing a thick trail of smoke out the side of his mouth. Realizing that he'd just exhaled on Jeff, the man quickly added. "And get my man here another one of whatever he's drinking."

Jeff offered the bartender a half-smile and gave the Budweiser a slight wiggle. "You're an attendant at the morgue." Jeff said. "On the night shift. That's where I know you."

"Yup. Harry Kane," the man said, extending a finely manicured hand toward Jeff. "But folks call me Candy." He took Jeff's hand before Jeff could properly extend it and gave it a quick but powerful squeeze. "And you're that French guy, right?" Candy asked, his hand still wrapped around Jeff's.

"Yeah. Jeff French. Nice to meet you."

The drinks arrived, allowing Jeff to retrieve his hand. There was something odd about Harry Kane's touch, as if the man's hand was too soft, too smooth. Jeff shuddered and polished off what was left in his beer. Harry Kane's hand had felt like a slug.

Candy shot back his Rock-n-Rye and ordered another. "So how do you like riding the Bony Express? That is one job I wouldn't want." Candy laughed and drummed his fingers against the top of the bar. "I know it gets crazy as shit sometimes at night."

Jeff shrugged. "It's not too bad. Dull mostly, but it can get kind of ugly sometimes."

Candy snorted twin streams of smoke from his nostrils "Yeah, you don't have to tell me about it. I've been tagging stiffs on the night shift for almost four years now. Ain't much in the way people croak that I haven't seen. One time, we got this guy who committed suicide by shoving a flare gun up his ass. Can you believe that? A fucking flare gun up the ass. That's got to take the cake for weird."

When Jeff didn't respond, Candy asked, "So, you planning on becoming a doctor or something?"

The question took Jeff by surprise. "A doctor. No. Why would you think that?"

The bartender brought a second Rock-n-Rye and a shot for Jeff that he couldn't remember ordering. Candy grabbed his shot but didn't drink it. "Well, a lot of times, college guys get jobs running ambulances or filing stiffs while they're in pre-med. They think that will give them some kind of bullshit experience when they get to med school. Those guys are always pricks." Candy sucked in another lungfull of smoke then crushed the half good cigarette atop the bar. "You got a look about you. Like you could be one of those college guys."

Candy said college guys as if he was chewing on a turd. "Not me," Jeff said with a laugh, which Candy interpreted as an invitation to pluck another smoke from Jeff's pack. "I'm really not one for school. But why do you think I look like the college type?"

Candy lit the cigarette, this time without the dramatic flair. "Well, it's not so much that you actually look like a college guy. It's just that you don't look like the usual kind of guy who drives the night shift. They're mostly burnouts or freaks." Candy paused for an almost imperceptible moment, but Jeff noticed it. "Like your partner."

EIGHT

The first night, Grace sang to him in his sleep. It was a soft, gentle song about a forgotten love whose memory had surfaced after a hundred years. Though Phil heard the song in a dream, he knew Grace Finster was speaking to him from the grave. She told him to wake up and put on the glasses he had stolen.

Phil did as he was instructed, and when he peered through the ill-fitting bifocals he saw the twin fates of heaven and hell. One in each lens. Through the left lens he saw an ecstasy of white, so perfect in its purity that Phil could never capture it in words or on canvas. Through the right lens he saw a chasm of flame and eternal darkness where tortured screams rose like smoke. All Phil had to do was adjust his focus or tilt his head and he would go from indescribable paradise to an inferno of the damned.

The sight was enough to drive him mad, but Grace Finster's voice came to him just as he was about to rip his eyeballs from his socket *You have been chosen*, she whispered. *Chosen to save our souls.*

Phil ripped the glasses off his face, but the voice of Grace echoed inside his head. *To save our souls, Phil. Can you do it?*

Weeping, Phil fell to his knees "I don't know," he cried out. "Whose souls am I supposed to save?"

Mine, came the answer. *And more, many more.*

NINE

"My partner?" Jeff asked surprised. "What's wrong with Phil?"

Candy laughed and swiveled on his stool to face Jeff. "You ever notice anything odd about Phil? He ever say anything weird?"

The image of Phil Luxor slipping the hearing aid into the pocket of his lab coat jumped into Jeff's mind. "He doesn't really say much," Jeff said. "Not much at all."

A smug grin stretched across Candy's face as if the skinny man knew Jeff was lying. "Is that so? Well, you just wait. Most of the guys who've ridden with him say he's nuts. Always talking about weird shit like art and where people go after they die. One guy, Chet, told me that Luxor told him how he liked to visit the graves of the people he picked up, just to see how they were doing in the afterlife. I'm telling you man, it's weird."

Jeff nodded, and for a moment considered asking Candy if he knew about Phil's collection, but decided against it. Instead, he asked Candy why everyone at the morgue called the ambulance he drove the Bony Express.

"Don't know," Candy said. "Phil Luxor started calling it that when he took over the night shift. Maybe it's because he thinks it's the fastest way to get to the bone yard."

Jeff accepted the answer and turned back to his drinks. The glass and the bottle, both empty now, still formed a triangle with the small pile of ones that was all that remained of Jeff's twenties. Father, Son, and Holy Ghost.

Jeff was getting tired. He'd have to go home soon, but he couldn't sleep. He couldn't risk that.

Jeff closed his eyes and allowed his chin to drop to his chest. From far away, he heard Candy asking him if he was all right. Jeff didn't reply. He just closed his eyes so tight that they started to burn behind his lids.

Staring back at him from the mirror was a woman with auburn hair and no face.

She was screaming.

TEN

Phil stared out the window from the studio of his twelfth-story apartment at the empty street beneath him and sighed. He was still pretty buzzed from the four bong hits he took when he first got home, but unlike most mornings, the dope didn't prove to be the inspiration he needed in order to get to work. Something was holding him back today. Something that wouldn't let him work. Artistic constipation Phil called it. Blocked up tighter than a drum. Absently, Phil rolled the hearing aid he had collected that morning between his fingers. It felt warm to his touch, vibrating softly. Henry Wallace had something to say, Phil was sure of that. But right now, he wasn't certain that he wanted to listen.

Phil turned from the window and stared at the enormous blank canvas in front of him. For once, he thought, he wanted to paint something without their help. Just take the brush and let his own creative genius work itself upon the canvas.

The thought made him laugh out loud. He was no way near stoned enough to convince himself he had a modicum of creative genius. Despite his self-proclaimed status as an artist, Phil was quite aware of the limits of his talent; genius was for others.

He held the hearing aid to his face and frowned. The humming continued which made Phil think of his new partner on the Bony Express. He was testing Jeff when he told him that the hearing aid was for his collection. Testing the new guy to see how curious he was.

But Jeff didn't take the bait. He pretended not to be interested in Phil's collection. But the indifference was an act, of that, Phil was certain. He could see it in Jeff's perfect blue eyes. Deep within their beauty and intelligence, they burned with curiosity. Yes, there was something different, something special about Jeff French.

Smiling, Phil set his coffee mug on his sofa and picked up a thick, used paintbrush off the floor. This painting is for Jeff, he thought, slipping Henry Wallace's hearing aid into his left ear. As soon as it came in contact with Phil's flesh, the hearing aid stopped vibrating and grew cold.

And Phil was inspired.

ELEVEN

It was nearly 11:00 am when Jeff left Candy at the bar and started back to his apartment. He drank up the two twenties he originally laid on the bar plus another five dollars worth of booze, yet he still didn't feel drunk. His new drinking partner, however, had downed half a bottle's worth of Rock-N-Rye and was well on his way to getting ripped. Since Candy had the evening off, he decided to remain at The Strand and get royally shit-faced. He suggested that Jeff call in sick and join him for an afternoon of drinking, but Jeff shrugged off the offer telling Candy that he was too new on the job to do that. "If you say so, man," Candy said. He plucked a pen out of his jacket pocket and scribbled on a spent pack of matches. "Home number's on top," he said, handing the pack to Jeff. "Cell phone is on the bottom. Call me if you change your mind."

"Thanks," Jeff said, slipping the pack into the ass pocket of his jeans. "I might do that."

But as he strolled down Pirl Street, past the boarded-up dry cleaners and the camera repair shop, Jeff knew he wouldn't call Candy. The last thing he needed now were friends. Even a casual drinking buddy could prove dangerous. He was alone now, and there was safety in isolation.

Hello my pretty one.

Jeff shook her voice from his memory and took the matchbook out of his jeans. Candy had written *Call me* above the numbers, a two word message Jeff had received hundreds of times before from an equal number of women and men who wanted a hell of a lot more out of Jeff than polite conversation. As Jeff stared at the message, memories of the life he abandoned just a few months ago came flooding back. Memories of faces and bodies that he had held and kissed. Bodies that he had become entwined and lost in the exquisite smoothness of their flesh. But these memories brought no nostalgic longing for the old days; no hunger to head back west to his old life.

Call me.

"If only you knew what a mistake that would be, Candy," Jeff said, ripping the matchbook into shreds and letting the pieces fall at his feet.

Jeff resumed his walk homeward, and as he did every morning, said a prayer that in those few hours he slept before another night of picking up the dead, he wouldn't dream. It was always so much worse when he dreamed.

TWELVE

For the next three days, the routine remained the same for Jeff. He and Phil drove the Bony Express and picked up the late-night dead, and in the early morning just after sunrise, Jeff would go to The Strand to drink. Before Jeff could finish his second beer, Candy would show up and bum a few cigarettes and do everything possible, short of coming out and saying it, to convey the fact that he wanted to take Jeff home and screw his brains out.

Jeff felt bad for Candy. Maybe at another time in another place he would have let Candy take him home. Like untold times before, he would have just closed his eyes and allowed himself to be devoured. Man, woman, it didn't matter. Sex was all the same, and for Jeff, it had never been a hassle.

But those days were gone; gone like her face.

"I don't know why you want to talk about him," Candy snapped when Jeff asked for more information about Phil Luxor. It was the third time the two men drank together, and Jeff could tell that Candy was growing possessive of his company. "I told you, he's supposed to be some kind of artist. Probably not a good one." The jealousy in Candy's voice was so thick Jeff nearly laughed.

"Why do you say that?" Jeff asked. "Have you ever seen his work?"

Candy shook his head. "No. But he used to talk about this big project he was doing called Metamorpho. He said it was going to make him famous. A star in the firmament of heaven." Candy started laughing. "I swear to Christ, that's what he said. A star in the firmament of heaven."

Jeff nodded and pushed his cigarettes closer to Candy. The gesture was met by quick smile. "So what ever happened to Metamorpho? Did he finish it?"

"Don't know," Candy said. "Last time he mentioned it was last year." He took up the pack and tapped out a fresh smoke. "And he sure as shit ain't no star in no fucking firmament of heaven."

Jeff looked into the mirror behind the bar and saw the faceless woman where his reflection should have been. Her head was whipping back and forth across the glass. "None of us are."

THIRTEEN

Four days later, Phil added to his collection.

It was a hairpin taken off of a 57-year-old widow named Stella Linkletter who had been murdered in her kitchen while doing the dishes. Being mostly deaf, Stella didn't hear the intruder enter her three-room apartment. She had her transistor radio in the kitchen turned up to full blast and was singing along with Bobby Goldsboro when she was impaled from behind. Dressed in her bathrobe and with her hair in curlers, Stella died clutching at her chest, desperately trying to hold in the blood that spurted into her sink. But it was no use. Dying, she watched the white, soapy bubbles turn an odd brown. But as the life poured out of her like dishwater flowing down the drain, Stella's last mortal thought was not of herself, but of whoever might find her. Always a woman who took pride in the meticulous care she gave her home, she died sorry that she wouldn't have an opportunity to tidy things up a bit. Though small, it would have been a consolation to her to know that the mess would be much less than she imagined.

Stella had been dead for over forty-eight hours when Phil and Jeff were called in to take her none-too-fresh-corpse to the morgue. Once again, it was Officer Lance Jacobs who greeted them at the door.

"Long time no see," Phil said when Lance ushered them inside. "I hear you got another one for me." Phil grinned and cocked his head toward his partner. "I mean us."

Lance cast Jeff a sideways glance and frowned. "It's

ugly, alright. Poor lady got it while she was doing the dishes. Been dead awhile, it seems."

"A ripe one," Phil said, but Officer Jacobs didn't seem to notice the joke. He just took the clipboard and hurriedly scribbled his name at the bottom.

Phil watched as the police officer signed off on the retrieval forms. Lance was not one who usually hurried a pick up, but Phil could tell that Lance was in one hell of a hurry to get the body of Stella Linkletter into the Bony Express.

"This is different, Phil. When you see her you'll know this one ain't right." For a second it appeared that Lance was going to say more, but he stopped and handed the clipboard back to Phil. "We're all done in there, so you can take her now." He paused, then added. "You know the routine."

Taking back the clipboard, Phil motioned for Jeff to pull the gurney closer to the kitchen. "All too well," he told Officer Jacobs.

This time the cop cracked a slight but sad smile and shook his head. "I'm gonna go into the hallway and get some fresh air," he said. "I don't know what it is but this one is giving me a real bad feeling." Jacobs cast a quick glance toward the kitchen. "It just stinks too much."

And for the first time, Jeff noticed it too. Beneath the smell of decaying flesh; beneath the scent of mold and three day old Lemon Pledge, was another smell. A subtle undercurrent that permeated the smell of death with its own unique perfume.

It was hatred.

Hello my pretty one.

Jeff turned to Phil and sniffed. "I know what he means," he said. "I can smell something too." Jeff inhaled again and shuddered. The odor was painfully familiar.

"Probably one of Lance's guys farted," Phil replied, slipping his hands into a pair of latex gloves. "Let's go. The dearly departed awaits."

With the scent of hatred still fresh in his nostrils, Jeff followed his partner into the kitchen. Stella hadn't been moved from the spot where she died face down on the kitchen floor. A thick, dirty chalk outline was crudely traced around the woman's body like a cheap, white aura. "Look at that," Phil said, pointing to what was left of the woman's back. The tone of his voice was low and oddly subdued. "Lance is right. This ain't normal"

Phil stepped to the side, allowing Jeff an unobstructed view of Stella's corpse. She was on her stomach, the right side of her face flat against the tiled floor. Though her arms were tight against her sides, Stella's bare legs were spread wide as if they had been swept out from beneath her. Her left foot, still in a fuzzy, purple slipper that looked like a dog, was twisted inward as if the ankle had been broken. Rolled up in a ball near her right shoulder was what was left of Stella's flannel housecoat. A ragged sleeve dangled over the side of Stella's face, covering her chin and left cheek. But her eye was still open, like some white marble staring in Phil's direction. And for a brief moment, Jeff thought the woman looked familiar.

"Look at her back," Phil said, though his gaze was fixed on Stella's vacant face.

Jeff looked to where Phil was pointing. Stella's back had been flayed open as if she was a giant cod, the white bumps of her spinal column fully exposed. Foot length husks of skin had been peeled off and draped over her rigid arms. Covering Stella's buttocks like a blanket were long strands of tissue-thin flesh. But being a small woman with a tiny ass, most of the extra skin spread off Stella's rear-end onto the floor barely concealing the faint square pattern of black grout. Jeff took another step closer to the body and swallowed hard. The smooth ridges of her spine were exposed, allowing Jeff to count each of her vertebrae.

"There isn't any blood," he said, turning to Phil. "Why

is that? There should be blood all over this place."

Phil pursed his lips and nodded. Jeff was right. Considering the damage that had been done to Stella, the kitchen should have been coated in crimson. "Pull the gurney in, and let's get this over with."

Needing no further encouragement, Jeff pulled the gurney into the cramped kitchen. Tossing a clean, white sheet over Stella's body, Phil moved toward her head, while Jeff positioned himself at her feet. Grabbing her ankles with his right hand, and hooking his left arm under her knees, Jeff was ready to lift when he noticed Phil staring at the mound of hair peeking out the top of the sheet. Phil's left hand was fiddling with something beneath the sheet. "What the hell are you doing?" Jeff whispered as Phil plucked his hand free of Stella's hair. In it he held a thin, brown bobby pin.

Jeff's eyes bulged at what Phil had collected. "Are you nuts?"

Phil pocketed the souvenir and commenced to slide his arms beneath Stella's shoulders. "I need it," he said, not looking at Jeff. But even with his face downcast, Jeff could see Phil's expression. It was troubled but excited. "I can't tell you now, but I will."

Jeff couldn't believe what he was seeing. "You'll tell me when we're done or I swear I'm going straight to Sessoms."

Phil nodded. "Deal. Now let's get her on the gurney and get out of here."

FOURTEEN

"Have you ever heard of Ovid's *Metamorphosis*?" Phil asked Jeff as he passed him the tightly packed bong. The two were in Phil's apartment sitting on the overstuffed couch in the north-end cubicle that served as Phil's living room. Though Jeff insisted, Phil refused to tell him why he had to take the hairpin from Stella's corpse until, as Phil said, they were on his turf. "After our shift, we'll go back to my place, and I'll be able to show you what I'm talking about. But until then, I can't talk about it. Okay?"

Jeff could tell the man was serious, so he didn't press the issue. "Okay, but if you blow me off, I'm going to tell Sessoms."

But true to his word, Phil didn't blow Jeff off. The pair had two more pickups that evening, and after dropping the last one off to Candy, Phil told Jeff it was time to go to his place. "You're not meeting me at the bar?" Candy asked, surprised. He glared at Phil, but the ambulance driver ignored him. "I thought we were going to meet."

"Not today," Jeff said, not acknowledging the hurt expression on Candy's face. "Maybe tomorrow."

"When?" Candy began, but stopped when Phil started for the door. Leaving Candy's question unanswered, Jeff hurried to Phil's side.

"I think he likes you," Phil said when Jeff caught up to him.

"Yeah, but he doesn't like you."

Phil grunted. "No biggie."

The pair hurriedly signed out for the morning then

gathered their personal belongings from the staff lounge and headed for Phil's car. The two spent the ten-minute drive in silence, but when Phil pulled into the parking lot of the Exeter Towers, Jeff let out a low whistle. "I've only been in town a few months," he said. "But I know this is one pricey place. How do you afford it?"

Phil shrugged. "I'm rich," he said. "That's all."

Jeff knew better then to ask Phil why he drove a morgue wagon if he was rich. There was no doubt in his mind that Phil Luxor was as eccentric as they come. "Must be nice," Jeff replied. In his mind's eye he pictured his own efficiency apartment that sucked up over half of his monthly paycheck in rent.

"Come on." Phil turned off the ignition and pushed open the driver's side door. "I live on the top floor."

When Phil opened the door to his apartment, Jeff was surprised to find himself in a tight, narrow corridor with walls less than a foot above Jeff's head. Jeff looked up and saw that the walls did not extend to the ceiling. "Did you do this?" Jeff said, motioning to the wall.

Phil nodded. "Yeah. This apartment is actually the whole top floor but it was too much open space for me. I don't like that, so I turned the loft into a bunch of smaller rooms. There are two doors into every room all connected by the plywood maze. I got the idea from watching The Shining. I think it's kind of cool." Phil ushered Jeff through the narrow maze of plywood walls to the living room. "Have a seat," Phil said, pointing to the sofa. "I'll go get us some beers." Before Jeff could answer Phil turned and was gone.

Jeff sighed and plopped himself down on Phil's couch. The living room was sparsely furnished, just an easy chair and a reading lamp beside the couch. Jeff glanced about, noticing that there was no television or stereo in the room. Probably has an electronics room, Jeff thought. He unzipped his jacket and decided that Phil's apartment was a bit too claustrophobic for his tastes.

Less than a minute later, Phil was back with a twelve pack of Corona and a silver-plated water bong. "I hope you don't object," Phil said, holding the bong aloft.

"Nope," Jeff replied, though it had been months since he last got high. "No objections at all."

"That's the spirit." Phil set the beer on the floor. As Phil sat on the couch and packed the bong, Jeff removed two beers from the package and opened them. He took a long swig, then seeing that Phil was finished packing the bong, handed him his beer. "It's good," he said. "Cold."

Exchanging the bong for the beer, Phil asked his question about Ovid's *Metamorphosis*.

"I think so," Jeff said before putting the bong to his lips. Phil produced a lighter and lit the bowl while Jeff inhaled.

"Really?"

Jeff nodded, keeping his mouth shut. He let the sweet smoke fill his lungs until they began to burn, then slowly, he exhaled. Perhaps the dope-free months had lowered his resistance to pot, because no sooner had he exhaled the first bong hit then the hazy mellow feeling of an impending buzz surfaced. Either that, or Phil Luxor was in possession of the best damn weed he'd ever smoked. Phil noticed the look on Jeff's face. "Good shit, isn't it? I got it from some kid in town named Espy." Phil took the bong and did his own quick hit. But unlike Jeff, Phil was practiced enough that he could still speak with his lungs full of marijuana smoke. "So you know about *The Metamorphosis*?"

"Yeah. When I was in high school, I had this one English teacher who made us read all these Greek and Roman myths. Most of the kids thought it was boring, but I kind of liked them. *The Metamorphosis* is some myth about the gods changing people into animals and things, right?"

Phil was impressed. "Something like that."

Jeff took a quick sip of his beer and eyed Phil sternly.

"So what's that got to do with you taking that hairpin off that dead lady tonight?"

"Everything." Phil took the hairpin out of his shirt pocket and held it in the palm of his right hand. "Let me explain *The Metamorphosis* first, then I'll show you what this is all about." Phil wrapped his fingers tightly around the hairpin. "Okay."

"Fine with me." Jeff took the bong and stoked up another bowl. The buzz was starting to creep up on him. It was a pleasant feeling that he'd long missed.

"I know Harry Kane has told you that I'm an artist, and that I've been working on a piece called Metamorpho."

"Yeah. He said it was going to make you a star in the firmament of heaven."

The embarrassed look on Phil's face told Jeff that the artist wasn't expecting him to know that. "Anyway, Ovid's *Metamorphosis* is a lot more than just a collection of ancient stories; it's a kind of mythological blueprint for the evolution of man and the universe from the beginning when everything was chaos through creation, and then the four ages of man."

"Sounds like heavy stuff," Jeff said before taking another bong hit.

"Very," Phil shot back. "And underlying the entire thing is the idea of eternal and constant change. Everything in the universe is in a constant state of metamorphosis, changing from one state to another. And that includes people."

Jeff nodded as he exhaled. "So? Isn't that what Darwin was supposed to be all about? Evolution being a part of the whole natural process."

"Not exactly. I'm not talking about evolution." Phil started to drum his fingers across his near-empty beer bottle. "What I'm talking about is the metamorphosis of the individual as the changes of life continue on into death."

Passing the bong back to Phil, Jeff pushed himself deeper into the oversized couch. "I still don't know what any of this has to do with art, or, for that matter, the stuff you've been taking off the corpses."

"Fair enough," Phil said, placing the bong on the floor. He grabbed two beers from the container and motioned for Jeff to get up. "Maybe if I show you, you'll understand."

Reluctantly, Jeff stood and followed Phil through the maze of his apartment to the gallery. The beer and bong hits coupled with the succession of quick turns Phil led him through made Jeff dizzy. By the time the two reached Phil's gallery, Jeff's head was spinning, and he needed to sit down. Noticing his friend's discomfort, Phil put his hand on his shoulder and guided him through the door. "Here we go," Phil said once the two were inside the room. "Ta-da."

Jeff took a few uneasy steps into the room and glanced around. Nearly every inch of wall space was covered with Phil's paintings, but they didn't reflect any artistic sensibilities in any sense that Jeff was familiar. The paintings, mostly portraits of various shapes and sizes, looked as if they had been done by a marginally talented child whose natural medium was black velvet canvas. Jeff quickly noticed that, besides lacking artistic merit, all the portraits shared a disturbing commonality. Regardless of the sex, the faces in all the paintings resembled effeminate versions of Phil Luxor.

Maybe it was the dizziness in his head or the lingering effects of the pot, but Jeff felt a sudden queasiness at the sight of Phil's collection. It was too disorganized, too much of a mixed match of obtuse colors and discordant styles that made Jeff feel as if he'd been sucked into an orgy of electric blues and purple. It was too many pairs of Phil Luxor's badly painted eyes staring at him from the walls.

"I know a lot of them are rather primitive," Phil said,

turning his back to Jeff. He casually walked about the room, inspecting his own handiwork. "But I think I finally have found my style as a portraitist. Sort of a cross between neoclassicism, Picasso, and Norman Rockwell."

His eyes clamped shut, Jeff imagined Phil to be the bastard son of Rockwell and Picasso. A sickly love child with too much time and precious little talent. The thought did little to ease Jeff's growing headache.

Phil tapped Jeff on his shoulder and motioned for him to look at a painting to Jeff's right. "That's one of the first pieces I did after becoming an ambulance driver. It's a man named Gary Kenny, my first pick-up."

Jeff opened his eyes and glanced at the painting. Dressed in a plain black tuxedo, Gary Kenny was a thin, awkward looking man with the slightly elongated and pouty face of Phil Luxor. "Why is he in a tux?" Jeff asked.

Phil shrugged. "Actually he had a heart attack while watching TV in his underwear. I just thought it would be nice to dress him up a bit. It doesn't matter. This is what I really wanted to show you," Phil said, pointing at the far end of the left-side wall. "These are the paintings I did based on Ovid's *Metamorphosis*."

Jeff turned, half expecting to be confronted with more of the same garishness, but what he saw was much different. It was a series of four paintings depicting a man undergoing a painful change from man to wolf. Unlike the clownish Phil-faced portraits that covered the rest of the gallery, these works demonstrated a mature handling of tone and color. Though he was no art critic, Jeff had been taken to more than his share of gallery openings, and these paintings were as good as anything he'd seen before. Jeff took a step forward and whistled between his teeth. "Damn," he said impressed. "These are good."

Phil could tell that Jeff was sincere in his praise. "Thanks. These are the only things in the gallery that I'm actually proud of. The rest of this stuff," he said, waving his arm in a semicircle at the opposite wall. "Is just a lot of wall filler."

"Tell me about these," Jeff said, not taking his eyes off the first painting in the series. It was of a handsome, brown-haired man in a tunic running through a plush, green meadow. The man is caught in mid-stride, his face partially turned as if looking over his shoulder for signs of a pursuer. His left arm is thrust in front of him, but instead of a hand, a vulpine paw extends from below the forearm. "Who is this?"

"It's Lycan," Phil replied. "He was some ancient Greek king. In *The Metamorphosis*, Zeus got pissed off at him and turned him into a wolf. It's where the word lycanthropy comes from."

"Lycanthropy?"

"Werewolves," Phil explained. "That's the technical term for turning into a werewolf."

Jeff nodded and examined the remaining paintings. In the second, Lycan has fallen to one knee, the left arm now fully transformed into a wolf's front leg. In the third painting, Lycan's limbs have all become that of a wolf, and the transformation has begun in his face. His hair is now longer and scraggly, and his nose and jaw have become elongated and more pointed. In the final painting, all traces of humanity have vanished from Lycan's form. He has been completely transformed into a wolf.

Not completely.

Jeff leaned forward and examined Lycan's wolfen face. Everything was perfect, except for the eyes. Lycan's eyes were still those of the man in the first painting. Only now, behind their pain they reflected an unimaginable fear. "He still has a man's eyes," Jeff said, pointing to the painting. "Why?"

"The eyes hold the soul," Phil said, inching closer to Jeff. "In the story, Lycan's true punishment is that he knows that he is a man trapped in a wolf's body. Unlike werewolves in the movies, Lycan was only a beast on the outside. In his head, in his soul, he knows that he is still human. And that's his real punishment. He spends the rest of his life lamenting his lost youth and beauty. He has nothing left but to howl in misery because he cannot escape what he has become."

Jeff nodded and glanced again at Lycan's sad, terrified eyes.

"Come on," Phil said. "There's more I want to show you."

Jeff took another moment to admire the quartet of paintings before turning toward the door. "I always thought art was a type of metamorphosis, a way of changing one thing into another," Phil said as he ushered Jeff out of the gallery and back into the plywood maze. "An artist takes raw materials and transforms them into something new. And for the longest time, I thought that was enough. But I came to realize that when my paintings or sculptures were done, they were no longer..." Phil stopped, struggling for the right word.

Jeff supplied it.

"Becoming."

"Exactly. They were no longer becoming something; they were finished. But don't you see, Jeff? If everything in the universe is going through a constant state of change, the very fact that my art was completed made it meaningless. Its very completeness made it foreign, something unnatural. Do you know what I mean?"

Jeff said he thought he did.

"Good." Phil had taken Jeff through three twists in the maze to a black door that opened to his studio. "So I was left with only one thing to do. Create a work of art that was in a continual state of metamorphosis."

"Metamorpho."

Phil opened the door. "Yes."

Jeff took one step into the room and stopped. "Good,

God," he said when he saw the thing in front of him. Expecting another painting, Jeff was stunned to discover that Metamorpho was more machine than art. At least five feet wide and seven feet high, Metamorpho was an intricate system of pulleys and wires surrounding a six-foot skeletal frame of a headless man. Made of metal pipe and chicken wire, the skeleton stood atop a square platform. Two rows of small, cast iron wheels at the bottom of the platform allowed Metamorpho to move back and forth. A system of counter balances attached to two pulleys allowed the machine to sway slightly from side to side. At the end of the skeleton's arms, broken pairs of reading glasses had been attached to serve as fingers. Glued to the fingers of the left hand was a paintbrush sopping with Van Dyke Brown. Jeff watched, amazed, as the arm jerked back and forth sending bits of brown paint flying off the brush onto an enormous canvas just inches out of the skeleton's reach. Covering the wall-length canvas were dozens of paint splotches of various sizes and hues.

"It's a machine," Jeff said, not able to take his eyes off the automaton.

"That and so much more," Phil agreed, entering the room. "It's also an artist." Phil pointed to the canvas. "Look," he said. "This is our work. His and mine."

Jeff moved forward to inspect the canvas. What appeared at first to be a collage of random splotches became more distinct. Dotting the canvas were hundreds of grimacing faces, each one projecting a moment of some intense private agony. Jeff moved closer, his gaze falling upon the face of a young woman painted in dark shades of red and violet. Two pinholes of black made up her eyes. As he stared, a drop of Van Dyke brown fell from the tip of Metamorpho's brush. When the paint touched her face, a subtle alteration came over it. Jeff leaned forward. Another bit of paint hit the face making it seem to elongate, its features growing sharper, almost vulpine like the painting of Lycan.

Unnerved, Jeff stepped back from the canvas. "What is this?"

Phil watched Metamorpho's brush pass over the other figures. "Like you said," Phil began. "They're becoming, changing from one thing to another. I paint their faces on the canvas and Metamorpho does the rest."

"Who are they?" Jeff asked. "And just exactly what are they supposed to be becoming?"

Phil turned to Jeff and shook his head. "You know who they are."

And Phil was right. As soon as he saw the tortured faces on the wall, Jeff knew he was looking at Phil's collection. "These are the people you've picked up in the Bony Express."

"Not all of them," Phil said. "Just some. Just the ones who talk to me."

"The ones who have talked to you?"

Phil shrugged, a slightly embarrassed grin coming to his face. "It's nothing, really. I just have this gift, I guess. But sometimes I can hear the dead."

Jeff wanted to laugh but the expression on Phil's face told Jeff that he was serious. "And what do the dead tell you? Paint my fucking picture."

Phil's grin grew wider. "Actually, yes." He motioned for Jeff to look at the bottom, right hand corner of the canvas. "This is a quote from Ovid's *Metamorphosis*. It sort of sums everything up."

Bending forward, Jeff noticed for the first time the soft hum of gears and a motor coming from the base of Metamorpho. Damn thing has a battery, Jeff thought. He laughed to himself as he read the quote. *Our souls are deathless; always, when they leave our bodies, they find new dwelling-places.* "So, what does it mean?"

"It means that, like our bodies, every soul is in a permanent state of flux, always moving from one thing to another. But not everyone's soul is ready to move on. Sometimes bits of the soul get left behind. The souls who talk to me aren't prepared to undergo their metamorphosis, so I paint their souls onto this canvas and Metamorpho completes their…" Phil paused, smiling. "Becoming."

Jeff shook his head and wished he had brought the bong with him. "So you built this machine-thing so the souls you've painted can become something else, right?"

Phil crossed his arms over his chest and nodded. "Some become other people. Others become animals or trees. Even grass." Phil moved closer to the metal skeleton. "Look closely, Jeff. Soldered into Metamorpho's frame are all the things I've collected from the dead. Eyeglasses, jewelry, watches. Look here," Phil said, pointing to a small, brown lump near what would have been the right shoulder. "Henry Wallace's hearing aid."

"But why?" Jeff asked.

"Because we leave behind tiny bits and pieces of who we are in everything we have. Our clothes, our furniture, even these bits of jewelry have traces of the souls of the people who possessed them. Sometimes, there's more than just a little bit of a soul trapped within them. They belong to people who haven't become yet. They're the ones I can hear. The one's I collect for Metamorpho."

"You see, Jeff. That hearing aid still has a part of Henry's soul in it, and it called to me. It asked for my help. I painted his face on the canvas, but it is Metamorpho that creates the becoming. Here," Phil said excitedly. "Look closer."

Reluctantly, Jeff moved within inches of the metal skeleton. What at first glance looked to be smooth metal piping, Jeff saw was pockmarked with dozens of ripples. Jeff could see soldered into the skeleton a number of coins and bits of glass. One shiny protrusion looked like half of a gold tooth. "The hairpin you took off the lady today," Jeff said, still examining the skeleton. "That will go on this too."

"Exactly. That hairpin has a bit of Stella's soul trapped in it. But once it becomes a part of Metamorpho, it adds to all the other bits of soul that are collected on him. That's the trade-off. Metamorpho helps them to become, and in turn, they give him a soul."

Jeff swallowed the urge to laugh by pouring a half bottle of Corona down his throat. The uneasiness he felt in Phil's gallery was returning. Turning, he noticed an easel in the corner of the room opposite Metamorpho. A heavy black tarp covered it. "What's that?" Jeff asked, waving his bottle at the covering.

Without looking, Phil called it the work in progress. "I'll show it to you when it's done."

"I've seen enough," Jeff said. He couldn't explain the sudden claustrophobia that gripped him, but he needed to get away from the headless metal man and back to the living room to smoke more dope. Not waiting for a reply, Jeff turned and headed out of the room.

Once he made it back to the couch, Jeff immediately started to pack the bong. "So you really think you hear the dead?" Jeff asked, as Phil came into the room.

"I do hear the dead," Phil replied. He cracked open another Corona and eyed Jeff coolly. "That is the truth. Now I told you my story, you tell me yours."

The request took Jeff by surprise. "Who says that I have a story?" he said, carelessly tapping the marijuana into the bowl. A healthy pinch of pot fell onto the couch. "Did the dead tell you that?" Jeff put the bong to his lips and stoked it up.

"Yes. Henry Wallace did. He said you're running."

Jeff laughed through a mouthful of marijuana smoke, but the sound that came from his throat was hollow and full of despair. "The corpse whose hearing aid you stole told you that I'm on the run. Oh man, that's fucking rich. Did he tell you what I'm running from?"

Phil shook his head. "He only said you were scared."

Hello my pretty one.

"So tell me, Jeff. Are you scared?"

The question hit Jeff like a blunt ax. He did have a story that he'd been keeping to himself for nearly a year, letting it gnaw at him like a hungry rat that had gotten its teeth into a nice chunk of cancerous tissue. If anyone were crazy enough to believe why Jeff was on the run, it would be the bohemian artist who talked to the dead. After all, Henry Wallace sure nailed it when he said that Jeff was scared.

"Okay, you want my story? You got it, but I don't think you're going to believe me. Hell, I don't even believe it most of the time, but you asked for it." Jeff took a deep breath and began.

"Have you ever heard of a guy named Scott South?"

Phil shook his head. "What is he, a rapper?"

"No. A porno actor."

Phil raised his eyebrows, a gesture that put Jeff in mind of Mr. Spock. "And I take it that you are this Scout South?" Phil asked, a thin smile creeping across his face. "A porno star with a past. Oh I knew this was going to be good."

"My name is Jeff French. Scout South was just my acting name. It's not who I was."

Phil slapped his knee and burst out laughing. "Oh, tell me. You aren't one of those guys with a 14 inch schlong, are you? Some kind of John Holmes clone?"

"Nothing so dramatic," Jeff replied, casting a casual glance toward his crotch. "Nine inches, nothing special."

Phil snorted. "Yeah, maybe not for you. But for the rest of us mere mortals . . ."

This time Jeff did laugh. "Anyway, my story. You still want to hear it?"

Phil told him to proceed.

"Okay. I got into the porn business on the west coast

about three years ago. I was never one of the really big porn names, but I had steady work doing three, maybe four pictures a week. Most of the directors I worked with liked me because I showed up to work on time, and I wasn't an asshole. Anyway, a year ago I was doing a picture called *Hard Attack* with a friend of mine named Lenny Congreve. It was an easy shoot, my only scene was a three-way with Lenny and this new chick." Jeff paused and took a swig of his beer. "Her name was Cindy Hart, but in the films she was called Kissy Mantrap. Nice name, huh?"

When Phil didn't reply, Jeff continued. "Anyway, it's a standard porn scene. Lenny and I are supposed to be T.V. repairmen who come over to Kissy's place and screw her in the living room. It was an easy scene, blocked out real simple. Nothing kinky, so Lenny and I would be out of there in about an hour with a grand apiece."

"A grand? You got paid a thousand dollars to have sex for an hour?"

Jeff shrugged his shoulders. "The money's good, but trust me, it's not as exciting as you think. It gets old real fast."

The look on Phil's face told Jeff that he didn't believe him

"Anyway, the director went over the scene with Lenny and me. Lenny was supposed to ring the doorbell and Kissy was going to let us in. Lenny and Kissy were supposed to have a few lines of dialogue before getting it on. I wasn't supposed to say anything; I was just supposed to stare at her. Kissy was going to be wearing nothing but a sundress, and she'd start by sucking face with Lenny. After they get started I was going to pay attention to her behind, and after about two minutes, Lenny would give me the sign to switch. Then she would do this little strip to get her dress off and we'd go to town. Like I said, the whole thing was pretty well-staged, but the weird thing was that Kissy wasn't there when the director went over the scene."

Phil shook his head and placed his hands in front of him in a show of mock surrender. "Wait a second. Are you telling me that the sex scenes in pornos are . . . choreographed?"

"Of course they are," Jeff said. "Do you think we could just make that shit up?"

That was a good point. Phil wasn't a big fan of porn, but he'd seen enough x-rated movies to know that the degree of sexual variety could hardly be johnny-on-the-spot.

"So the first time Lenny and I see Kissy, the camera is rolling on a live take. We're standing in the exterior set in our repairman costumes, and I ring the doorbell." Jeff stopped and took another swig. "Kissy opens the door and tells us to come in. She wasn't the most gorgeous woman I'd done a scene with, but she was hot. About five foot six with long red hair and a face that looked like it was sculpted out of marble. There was something odd about her, exotic almost. I'm telling you she was as white as could be. Except for her eyes. They were green, but a weird green like they were on fire."

"Anyway, she invites us in and we start our scene. Lenny and her start things off, then she's doing me, and then she's doing Lenny. Back and forth like the director wanted, and she didn't miss a beat. Like a real pro, she just went between Lenny and me for about twenty minutes, then it was time for the money shots."

Phil held his hand up. "Money shot?"

"The cum shot, Phil." Jeff said patiently. "It's where we ejaculate on the girl."

"Oh," Phil said, slightly embarrassed that he wasn't familiar with that particular phrase.

"So Lenny and I are in what's called the double-dare. That's where one guy's screwing the chick from behind while the other guy's getting a blowjob. Lenny was the one getting head and since he's the bigger name, he's supposed to come first. After he's done I'm supposed to do a ten count and blow my load."

"Jesus," Phil said visibly impressed. "You can do that on command? Just count to ten and ejaculate?"

Jeff shot Phil an annoyed glance. "That's why we're professional, Phil. Anyway, this is where it gets weird. Lenny does his bit, but the whole time, Kissy is looking at me and smiling. Just looking at me like she's not even aware of what Lenny's doing. It was weird, but I'd been with enough chicks not to be too surprised. So when Lenny's done I start my count, but before I can get to three she starts laughing. Not that phony porno grunting shit; she was laughing like she knew some big secret that the rest of us didn't."

"Then I noticed her eyes. They were black. Solid, like some kind of black stone. When I saw those I started screaming bloody murder. Then I ran. I mean I just ran like hell. Everyone was looking at me like I'd gone nuts, but I just grabbed my T.V. repairman duds and took off. I wasn't even worried about my money. I just knew if I didn't get away from that woman and her black eyes, I would go nuts."

"Did you?" Phil asked. "Get away from her?"

Jeff shook his head. "Not really. The next day Lenny called me and wanted to know why I freaked out. He tells me that the director is royally pissed off at me and saying that he'll never use me in any of his movies again. I told Lenny not to worry about it. That I just started feeling sick, and that I'd head over to the set that afternoon and apologize and straighten things up. I was lying through my teeth, but Lenny didn't know that. He told me to come by his apartment before I headed over to the set. He said he had this big surprise for me. I thought he might have gotten my money, so I headed over to his place."

"Lenny lives in this first floor apartment in Hollywood. Real nice place, and he's one of the more popular guys in the business, so there's usually a party going on there. But when I got to his place, there wasn't anyone around. Thinking about it now, that's the first time I'd ever been to his place and there wasn't someone hanging out. But back then, I didn't think anything about it. His door was open, and I just walked inside."

Phil brought the tips of his fingers to his lips and nodded slightly. "What did you find?"

"Nothing at first. I mean, Lenny was always a clean freak and his apartment was spotless. And that's the way it was when I walked in. I called out for him, but he didn't answer so I looked around the apartment. Finally I went into the bedroom. That's where I found him."

"Let me guess," Phil interrupted. "He was dead."

Jeff grunted and shook his head. "More than dead. Lenny was on the bed, just lying on his back. For a second I thought he was asleep, but then I take another step into the room, and I can see that his chest is ripped open and his insides are gone. Just ripped out. His eyes, too, are gone. He's just got these two empty holes in his head. I nearly puked, and I'm scared shitless when I see this, but instead of getting the hell out of there, I go over to the bed for a closer look because I noticed something else."

"What was that?"

"Lenny's got a hard on," Jeff said blankly. "His guts are ripped out, yet his dick is standing up at attention."

"That's not possible," Phil said. "At least I don't think it is."

Jeff shook his head. "It's not possible, trust me, I know. But yet there's Lenny with no eyes and a fucking boner. It was the weirdest thing."

"What did you do then?"

"Well, I'm standing there just looking at Lenny's dick when I realize there's no blood anywhere. Lenny's chest is ripped open but there ain't a spot of blood in the entire bedroom. Nothing on the bed, nothing on the sheets.

Everything was completely clean."

Jeff paused. From the brief, uncomfortable expression that passed over his face, Jeff knew that Phil was thinking the same thing he was. "Yeah, just like that lady we found tonight."

"Anyway, I decided I'd seen enough, so I start backing my way out of the room when Lenny's phone rings. I nearly shit myself when I heard it. I froze when Lenny's answering machine picked it up. I don't know why I didn't just get the hell out of there, but when I heard Lenny's voice telling the caller to leave a message after the beep, I just couldn't get my legs to move. Then I heard her."

"Who?"

"Who else? Kissy Mantrap. She was on the other end of the line, but she wasn't calling for Lenny. She was calling for me. She said that she was sorry our first encounter ended the way it did, and that she wanted to make it up to me. She said that she would come over to my place in an hour and we could talk."

"Shit," Phil said beneath his breath. "Was she watching the place? Waiting for you to show up?"

"That's what I thought at first, but I don't think so now. I mean, she knew I was there, but I don't think she needed to be watching Lenny's pad to know that. I think from the moment I met her, she's known everything I ever did. Everything I feel."

Cradling his head with his palms, Jeff sighed. "She's not a person, Phil. That's for damn sure. She's some kind of thing. Some kind of creature that fucks and eats men."

"And you think she killed Lenny?"

"Oh, I know she did. Killed him and ate his insides."

Phil thought for moment then eased himself back further into his chair. "Succubus," he said.

Jeff took his hands from his face and shot Phil a confused look. "Huh?"

"Succubus," Phil repeated. "It's a female demon with

an insatiable sexual appetite. She gets energy from sucking the life-energy out of men while she's screwing them. From what you've described of this Kissy Mantrap, she's a succubus."

Jeff shook his head. "I didn't know they had a name for what she is. But yeah, I guess so. Because I know she ripped open Lenny while he was screwing her"

"You know that for fact," Phil said.

Jeff wasn't sure if that was a question or a statement. "Yeah, I know for sure. She came to my apartment an hour later like she said she would and tried to do the same to me."

"Tell me," Phil said, eager for the story.

FIFTEEN

When Kissy Mantrap finished her message, a thousand impulses erupted in Jeff's brain telling him to run, screaming at him to grab some cash and a toothbrush and make like a tree and leave. Every inch of skin on his body, every strand of hair and drop of blood told him that what gutted Lenny was on its way over to do the same thing to him. Rip his eyes out and eat his insides.

No doubt about it.

But a small sliver of his subconscious overruled the rest of his body and told him there wouldn't be any use in running. It wouldn't matter where he went, she would know. And she would find him. Whatever Kissy Mantrap was, Jeff was certain of one thing.

She would find him.

In fact, that same sliver of brain told Jeff that Kissy fully expected him to run. Hoping that he would. It was the chase she loved. Tracking down her prey over weeks and miles, giving him just enough room to believe that he had actually escaped.

It was the part of the game she enjoyed most.

That's why Jeff stayed. It was the only chance to surprise her. To survive her.

But if he was to lay a trap for her, Jeff had to think fast. He had a gun back at his apartment, a big-ass Smith and Wesson he bought from a junkie for twenty bucks and three rocks of crack. Jeff wasn't into guns, but he had spent too many years on the street not to know the value of a little protection.

The first thing Jeff did when he got back to his apartment was to take the gun out of the footlocker he kept at the side of his bed. He slipped six bullets into the chamber and placed it on his bureau knowing that somewhere on the streets of Hollywood, Kissy Mantrap was just thirty hungry minutes away.

And that's when Jeff realized her weakness. She was a huntress, a creature of appetite who fed and fucked. Jeff pictured Lenny's erection, still poised in death as if bragging that it had been inside Kissy Mantrap. But, Jeff realized, it would not have been enough for Kissy. No man could ever be enough for Kissy Mantrap, and that's why she devoured them. Because in the end they couldn't fulfill her, they couldn't satisfy her.

Not completely.

And that left her hungry.

Jeff grabbed the mattress off his bed and dragged it into the living room. He knew what he had to do; it was so clear now. No man could ever fulfill the thing that was Kissy Mantrap, but unlike Lenny, at least Jeff knew he was playing with a stacked deck ahead of time. At least Jeff had time to prepare and maybe give her a little more than she expected. And maybe that little bit more would be just enough to catch her off guard.

Jeff flung the mattress in the middle of the living room, then brought out three pillows and arranged them at the head of the bed. He brought the gun from the bedroom and laid down on the mattress, his head square in the middle pillow. Letting his right hand dangle over the side of the mattress, Jeff stuffed the gun beneath it. Then he got up, straightened the pillows and the lone sheet and went back to his bedroom. Sitting on the bare box spring, Jeff opened the middle drawer of his bureau and took out a thin plastic tube and a baggie containing four grams of cocaine. Glancing at the clock above his bed, he saw that he had twenty minutes before Kissy was to arrive. Just enough time, he thought, ripping open the plastic bag. He didn't bother with the formality of cutting up lines of coke on a mirror; he just dumped it onto his bureau and rolled up a ten-dollar bill and started snorting it into his nostrils.

The impact of the coke hit him right away, but Jeff's mind was racing too fast to appreciate the instant buzz that gripped him. Jeff did another massive line of coke then stripped off his clothes. When he was naked, he started snorting again. Almost immediately the euphoric feeling washed over him, and with that came the cocaine erection.

Anyone in the porn business can tell you that the myth of the cocaine erection is no myth at all. Just a few lines of coke can turn any man's erection into a slab of unfeeling iron capable of standing at attention for as long as the cocaine held out. For the next fifteen minutes Jeff inhaled coke as his penis bulged to almost epic proportions. It throbbed painfully, then grew numb, becoming a useless appendage. When the cocaine was gone, Jeff took the tube and squeezed its contents into his right palm. It was a colorless, odorless goo called Man-De-Lay that promised, when used properly, to maintain a man's erection for over an hour. Jeff used it on two occasions when he had to do scenes with hangovers, and in both cases Man-De-Lay lived up to its billing. Jeff slathered a fistful of the goo onto his member and headed for the living room.

SIXTEEN

"Sweet Jesus," Phil said as Jeff paused his story long enough to take another bong hit. "You just waited there for her with a hard-on in hand."

Jeff laughed, brushing aside the reefer smoke with a quick wave of his hand. "Something like that. I laid down on the bed and waited. About a minute later the door opened. No knock, it just opened. I thought that seeing me naked with a hard on might take her by surprise, but it didn't. She just walked into the apartment wearing the same green sundress and said . . .

SEVENTEEN

"...hello, my pretty one."

"I know what you did to Lenny," Jeff said when he saw her.

Kissy Mantrap nodded once, then without ceremony lifted her sundress over her thin shoulders. She was naked beneath the dress, and as she tossed it on the floor next to the mattress, Jeff was surprised to see just how unspectacular her body was. Except for the pale, whiteness of her skin, Kissy Mantrap's body was firm and curvaceous in all the right places, but in the porn business, it was hardly one that would have stood out. It was her face, Jeff realized. The cold, emotionless face of a statue that made her irresistible. Jeff stared at the fine, smooth contours of that beautiful face and longed to kiss it.

"And you didn't run. Why is that my pretty one?" Kissy asked, stepping onto the mattress. She positioned herself so that she straddled Jeff's knees then gazed down at him as if she expected an answer.

Jeff's eyes traveled up her long legs and thighs, pausing briefly at the trimmed patch of auburn hair that came to a triangle between her legs. He didn't think it was possible, but the sight of her genitalia made Jeff's erection even stronger. His gaze lifted upward past her smooth, taut stomach and breasts until it became fixed on her cold, black eyes. A wave of fear gripped Jeff, and he nearly went for the gun. It was only with the greatest of effort that he kept his composure. "It wouldn't have done any good if I ran, would it?"

Kissy paused and rested her hands on her thin hips. "No, it wouldn't have. Wherever you would have gone, I would have found you. Sooner or later, I would have you."

Jeff swallowed hard before asking his next question. "What are you?"

Kissy's face remained emotionless, almost passive. "I'm a feeder," she said, her unblinking eyes still fixed on Jeff's. "That is the only way I can describe what I am in terms you would understand. I do not know who made me or why, I just know that I am, and it is my nature to feed. We are not all that much different, your kind and mine. It is just that my kind is much older than you could ever imagine."

"We're nothing alike," Jeff said. "You feed on people, on men."

Kissy shrugged and the ghost of a smile came to her face. "I feed on men, I feed on women. It is all the same to me. But don't you see, that is where we are a lot alike. You are not particular who you fuck for money. Men, women. It is all the same to you."

"I don't murder people."

Kissy laughed. "No you don't do anything that dramatic. Your kind just takes women and turns them into unfeeling lumps of flesh. You fuck them and take away their identity, their soul and over time that eats up tiny bites out of their spirits until there's nothing left. I feed on flesh and you feed on the soul, and that, Mr. South, is much, much worse." As she spoke, Kissy's left leg brushed against Jeff's thigh. At the touch of her flesh, a surge of electricity shot up Jeff's leg as if he had stepped on a live wire. Jeff's hips arched upward, instinctively drawn toward the woman above him. And as the fire spread through his torso and burnt itself out in his brain, Jeff knew at that moment, he wanted Kissy Mantrap more than any other woman he'd ever known.

"Why," Jeff asked, his breath coming in short gasps.

"Why me? Why Lenny?"

"Isn't that obvious," Kissy said, glancing down at Jeff's erection. "You have what I want. And besides." Kissy lowered herself onto her knees "You're so tasty."

Before Jeff realized what was happening, Kissy Mantrap thrust her torso forward and ground her hips against Jeff's. Though she looked as if she weighed no more than a hundred pounds, Jeff felt a crushing weight bearing down on his pelvis.

Once straddled across Jeff, a sound filtered out of Kissy's throat that was part moan and part growl. She threw her head back and dug her fingers into the slightly fleshy sides of Jeff's hips until five trails of blood seeped onto either side of the mattress. In a frenzy, she painfully bucked and ground her hips against Jeff's.

With every ounce of self-control he possessed, Jeff forced himself to remain rigid, his eyes clamped shut as Kissy Mantrap growled and humped him with an insane fury. He didn't dare look at her sculpted face for fear that seeing it would make him want to come. Instead he conjured up a parade of images that he knew would weaken his desire. He pictured rotting corpses strewn about the beach and ancient nuns wiping their withered, flabby asses in public. He thought of herds of pigs running into rivers, and coyotes falling off of cliffs. And for nearly thirty minutes he was able to stave off ejaculation, and as each minute passed, Jeff could sense that Kissy Mantrap was both surprised and impressed. From the sound of her satisfied grunts that sounded more bestial than human, Jeff knew that he was taking her farther than any man had taken her before. But even for someone with hundreds of porn credits to his stage name, Jeff, unlike the thing banging the snot out of him, was still human and could only hold out for so long. After a half hour of insane grinding, the cocaine and prolonging gel started to lose their effects.

When a familiar tingling sensation began deep in his prostate, Jeff knew he was just seconds from orgasm. And if he came, he knew he would end up like Larry. If he was going to survive, he had to act.

As Kissy's hips continued their furious grinding, Jeff let his right hand slip off the mattress and onto the floor. As casually as a man in his position could, Jeff inched his fingers beneath the mattress until he was able to wrap his hand around the grip of the pistol. But as he was pulling the gun from out of its hiding place, Kissy's frenetic grinding slowed. Gripping the pistol, Jeff looked for the first time at the woman atop him, only now there was little about her that could be called human. Her thin body still resembled that of a woman, but it had lost its smooth whiteness and was now a pale, reptilian gray. The round, firm breasts that had first caught Jeff's notice on the set of *Hard Attack* were replaced by what looked like porous twin bricks with small trails of green veins snaking beneath twin black nipples.

Jeff's eyes traveled up the length of Kissy's torso to the hideous mask that was her face. Gone were the exotic, sculpted features, replaced by a twisted mass of gray misshapen flesh and angles. Small black bumps covered her taut skin like open sores, stretching from her forehead to the scaly lump that bore a passing resemblance to a nose. Kissy's lips were peeled back, stretched to where her ears met two bulbous cheeks. Two sharp rows of finger-length teeth filled the enormous cavity of her mouth. A thick purpled lump of flesh Jeff imagined to be a tongue hung out the right side of the gaping maw, a thick glob of drool dangling from its tip.

The pressure on the side of Jeff's hips subsided as Kissy flung her head back and spread her arms out in front of her. The nails that had been ripping Jeff's flesh now resembled serrated strips of bone jutting from the clawed tips of what used to be Kissy's hands. Her claws clacked together as a sound Jeff had heard countless times in his colorful career as a sex worker drifted out of Kissy's deformed mouth.

She was moaning in pleasure.

Good God, Jeff thought. She's coming.

Using the muscle control that had served him so well in the porn industry, Jeff staved off his own building orgasm until he was sure Kissy was about to climax. An agonizing minute later, the thing atop Jeff stopped its grinding and tossed about the wild mane of auburn hair that had been spared the transformation from woman to beast. Mouth agape, Kissy growled in ecstasy as the first waves of orgasm struck her. And as she came, Jeff swung the gun beneath Kissy's chin.

Then Kissy's eyes flew open, and despite their empty blackness, Jeff could see a mixture of pleasure and shock behind them. And, he imagined, some perverse version of love.

Which was enough to make Jeff climax.

And as he came, Jeff fired all six shots into the throat of Kissy Mantrap, blasting her head off her shoulders even as he filled her with his seed.

EIGHTEEN

"You killed her while you were having an orgasm," Phil said, both horrified and fascinated at what Jeff had just told him. "Sweet Jesus."

Jeff leaned forward on the couch and sighed. Telling his story had been an uncomfortably sobering experience. "I shouldn't have told you," he said, quickly adding. "But you don't believe me anyway, do you?"

Phil shook his head. "The exact opposite actually. I believe every word of it."

An uneasy silence followed where Phil struggled to find the words to tell Jeff what Henry Wallace had whispered to him. "You shouldn't," Jeff finally said. "Nobody should."

Instead of answering, Phil stood up and motioned for Jeff to follow him back to the cubicle that housed Metamorpho. When they got there, Phil headed for the draped canvas. "The work in progress," Jeff remarked as Phil went to remove the tarp.

"The first night you asked about my collection," Phil said, pointing to Metamorpho. "That was the night I took Henry Wallace's hearing aid. I put it in my ear and it told me to paint a picture for you."

"For me?"

"Yes," Phil said softly. "By special request."

Phil pulled the tarp off the canvas, revealing the work in progress, the surreal portrait of something with a twisted demonic grin on a woman's face; something with flowing auburn hair and a green sundress who stretched her arms outward as if waiting for an embrace. A painting that only moments before, Phil discovered, was a not quite finished portrait of the thing that called herself Kissy Mantrap.

NINETEEN

Ignoring the No Smoking sign in the lobby of Jeff's apartment building, Phil lit a cigarette then tossed the spent match onto the floor. The action earned a disapproving look from an old lady waiting for the elevator, but Phil didn't care. He took a long drag then blew the smoke in the direction of the elevator before making his way out of the building.

Ever since Jeff told him about Kissy Mantrap, Phil's mind was consumed by a single thought. But before he could act on it, he had to make sure Jeff was all right. His reaction to the portrait of Kissy Mantrap was not what Phil expected. Jeff simply gazed on the painting for a few moments then turned to Phil and said he wanted to go home.

"That's it?" Phil shot back. "That's all you have to say?"

Jeff stood mute, not looking at the painting.

"I get messages from a dead guy to paint this monstrosity whom you've fucked and killed, and all you have to say is that you want to go home. Don't you think this is all a bit weird?"

Jeff lowered his head and looked at the floor. "You shouldn't have painted this, Phil," Jeff said. "I took her face away, and now you brought it back. You brought her back." A solitary tear fell from Jeff's eye onto the smooth, tiled floor. "Now take me home, Phil." Turning before Phil could answer, Jeff hurried out of the room. Dumbfounded Phil turned to the grinning horror trapped on the canvas.

"What did you do to him?"

But Kissy wasn't about to divulge any of her secrets.

"You bitch," Phil hissed at the painting, then hurried to catch up with Jeff.

TWENTY

Though Phil tried to get him to talk about the painting, Jeff remained silent. There really wasn't anything for him to say. The ugliness that he destroyed had been brought back. Not in form, but the image was enough to burn itself into the forefront of his mind. It stuck there like a scar, a deformity that once unmasked, could never be ignored. During the ride from Phil's place to his apartment, Jeff kept sneaking peaks of himself in the rearview mirror. The grinning, demon face of Kissy Mantrap stared back.

TWENTY-ONE

Phil's car was parked right outside of Jeff's building, but the artist hurried past it. Fortunately for him, Jeff lived dead center in the seediest part of town surrounded by dozens of dive bars, adult novelty shops, and a booming drug trade. Now that he knew of Jeff's past, Phil guessed that the red-light district probably felt like home for the ex-porn star.

Phil bypassed a pair of hookers looking for early trade and headed straight for the first adult bookstore he came to. It was in the third bookstore that he found what he was looking for. There he paid an overweight cashier named Bob twenty dollars for the store's lone copy of *Hard Attack*.

Hugging the videotape to his chest, Phil hurried to his car.

TWENTY-TWO

Jeff opened his eyes to find himself surrounded by darkness. Beneath his bare back and arms, Jeff felt the soft fabric of flannel sheets. I'm home, he thought. How he got there was a mystery, though. The last thing he could remember was Phil unveiling the portrait of Kissy Mantrap.

The work-in-progress.

Jeff took a long, slow breath. With the air came an odd mixture of gunpowder, cigarettes, and cheap perfume, a scent that made him think of Stella's apartment. It was definitely the smell of hatred, mixed with an undercurrent of desire.

Jeff pushed himself into a sitting position. In front of him came a rustling sound. "You're here, aren't you?" he said into the darkness.

The rustling came closer.

"You found me."

Hello my pretty one.

The words came so low and soft that Jeff wasn't certain if he had heard them or only thought them. But it didn't matter. Kissy Mantrap had found him. Whatever she was, six bullets into the head wasn't enough to kill her. Oddly, Jeff felt a strange sense of relief knowing that his death was moments away. He calmly reached over to the nightstand on the right side of the bed and flicked on the light.

Perched at the end of his bed was Kissy Mantrap. Lacking only stone wings, she looked like an auburn-haired gargoyle. Behind her stood the skeletal frame of

Metamorpho.

"You're here to kill me," Jeff said, staring into the black pools that were Kissy's eyes. "Just like you did Lenny."

Kissy shook her head slowly from side to side. "No, Scott South. I'm not here to kill you. Punish you, yes. Kill you, no."

"Don't call me that," Jeff shouted. "That's not my name."

"Maybe not," the thing replied. "But it is who you are and we cannot escape who we are, can we? We may change our names and faces, but we carry our hungers with us forever. I am an eater of men and you are a petty whore who longs for the feeling of flesh against flesh. Don't you, Jeff? Miss the touching, the kissing, the licking? Don't you miss me?"

Jeff tossed the covers off his legs and sprung out of bed. "No! That's not true. I got away from all of that when I got away from you!"

"But you didn't," Kissy said. "The desire is still there. The never-ending hunger." Spreading her arms out to the side, Kissy offered Jeff a full view of her naked, upper body. Jeff stood transfixed at the sight, unable to take his eyes off her rough leaden breasts. He was seized with a sudden, powerful urge to caress them, to run his fingertips and tongue along their cracked surface. He took two steps toward Kissy then stopped. The succubus chuckled and folded her arms over her chest. "We're the same, Jeff. We've both fed on flesh, and we like it. We just have separate appetites. You fuck without emotion, I feed without emotion. What's the difference?"

"I killed you," Jeff said, his voice barely registering a whisper.

"No. You can't kill me, Jeff. Just like you can't kill the hunger that lives inside you. I am that hunger, pretty one. That darkness that lives in everyone who craves flesh. We are eternal. All you did was take away my pretty face. But you're going to help me find it again, aren't you? You're going to help me be pretty again." Kissy laughed and hopped off the bed. "Come, my new friend has something to show you." Kissy hooked a clawed hand around Jeff's left arm and pulled him toward Metamorpho. "I know you two have met."

With her free hand, Kissy snapped her claw like a castanet. At the sound, Metamorpho took a lumbering step forward. "Look, Jeff. No gears, no pulleys. Your artist friend has succeeded in creating a living statue."

"No," Jeff said, trying to pull himself free. "It's a machine. It's not alive."

The grip tightened until Jeff thought his arm might snap in two. "But it is alive. Filled with all the shards of souls your friend collected." Kissy threw her head back and laughed. "That fool. He thought his masterpiece was saving the damned, helping their souls to become something else. Giving them new life. Well look at it, Jeff. This is the only thing those souls have become. Pieces of a monster trapped in their own private hell of metal. Now look!" Kissy shoved Jeff forward, sending him into the waiting arms of Metamorpho. "Look at his body," Kissy hissed. "Look at what has become of the souls your friend collected."

Realizing that he could not escape the statue's grip, Jeff did as Kissy instructed. He bent his head forward and examined the souvenirs that Phil had stolen from the dead. When he first examined Metamorpho's frame at Phil's apartment, the bits of eyeglasses and coins soldered onto it appeared to be little more than oddly spaced raises and bumps along the statue's smooth metal surface. Now that smooth surface erupted in dozens of open sores that oozed a viscous substance that was too dark and oily for blood. Jeff stared at one golf ball sized eruption on Metamorpho's chest where half of a quarter had been soldered. Only now the quarter was desperately trying to free itself. It quivered against the metal frame trapping it, the half visible face of George Washington writhing in agony. As Jeff stared, Washington's mouth opened, his lips peeled back in a silent, but agonizing scream.

"There is no metamorphosis, no 'becoming' for these people. There is only pain. Pain and the knowledge that their suffering is what gives this creature life. That is their true agony, Jeff, the knowledge that they have provided this monstrosity with appetite."

Jeff shut his eyes. "They're dead," Jeff whispered. "You can't hurt them."

"They are still in hell," Kissy said. There was no malice or gloating in her tone. It was a statement of fact. "Your friend damned those people."

His eyes still closed, Jeff felt Kissy stroke the back of his head with one of her clawed hands. At last, he thought. Enough of the bullshit, Kissy was done playing and was ready to rip his head off.

But the expected decapitation didn't happen. Instead, Metamorpho let him go.

"Look," Kissy said when Jeff was released. "A little visit to yesterday."

Jeff opened his eyes to find himself in the living room of an unfamiliar apartment.

But it wasn't unfamiliar; he had been there once. Recently.

From behind a closed door at the point where the combination living room/dining room emptied into the kitchen, a high-pitched voice was singing an old Bobby Goldsboro song. Instinctively, Jeff knew he was inside the apartment of the woman whose corpse he and Phil had removed earlier in the day. The lady named Stella.

Only now, she wasn't dead.

But she would be.

Jeff ran through the kitchen door as Stella's sing-along version of "Honey" came to a violent end. As Jeff flung himself into the kitchen, Metamorpho was hoisting Stella into the air, his metal arms shredding the terrycloth fabric of her housecoat, and ripping open her back. Jeff gasped as the tips of Metamorpho's eyeglass frame fingers poke through the soft flesh of Stella's throat just above the collarbone.

"No!" Jeff wailed. He started toward the headless monstrosity that was skewering Stella, but a stone-like hand clamped itself on his shoulder and pulled him back.

"Let him finish," Kissy's voice sounded in Jeff's ear.

Jeff struggled against Kissy's grasp but couldn't free himself. Though he couldn't see her, the scent of Kissy Mantrap filled the room. It was a dark fusion of cheep perfume and rotting flesh, the smell Jeff recognized as hatred.

No, not hatred.

Evil.

Helpless, Jeff watched as Stella writhed against the statue's metal frame, her frail arms and legs twitching wildly in the air. Thin geysers of blood squirted out of Stella's throat in time with her heartbeat spraying the walls and floor. That's not right, Jeff thought as the carnage continued. There wasn't any blood when we picked her up.

When life mercifully left Stella a minute later, Metamorpho tossed the woman's corpse to the floor and took a few steps back. "Time to feed," Kissy said, thrusting Jeff toward the bloodied carcass in front of him. "Yum, yum, yum."

His shoulders clamped in the vices that were Kissy's claws, Jeff shot a quick glance at Metamorpho. The blood that coated the lower half of the statue's arms was being sucked into the open wounds where the individual pieces of Phil's collection were soldered. "Yes," Kissy said. "Like anything with a soul, it must feed."

Grabbing Jeff's collar with her left claw and his belt with her right, Kissy thrust Jeff into the air and held him over Stella's body. From the twin holes ripped into her back, the warm stench of shit and decay filtered upward. Jeff gagged from the smell, but he couldn't take his eyes off the fleshy pulp of Stella's back. And as he dangled over Stella, Jeff understood what had become of her blood and internal organs.

"We all must feed," Kissy said, dropping the former porn star.

TWENTY-THREE

Jeff screamed, the coppery taste of warm liver fresh in his mouth.

"Wake up, Jeff," a voice said at his side. "You're having a bad dream."

A soft hand gently pressed itself on Jeff's bare shoulder and carefully shook him. His head was pounding and his throat felt as if the devil had pissed in it. "Where am I?" Jeff asked, opening his eyes.

The hand on his shoulder slipped forward and cupped the hard roundness of Jeff's pectoral muscle. "You're at my place. Don't you remember? You came here yesterday afternoon."

Jeff shuddered. The voice belonged to Candy.

"I thought you were drunk," Candy continued. "With all that raving about Phil Luxor and his statue. I swear to God, you were going on like some kind of crazy man." Candy lifted his long fingers and began to trace them up along the thin path of hair that ran down the middle of Jeff's chest. "I didn't think you were interested in me," Candy laughed. "You sure proved me wrong." The hand found its way back to Jeff's pec. "I think I'm going to be sore for days."

Brushing Candy's hand aside. Jeff pushed himself into a sitting position. He didn't have to remove the damp sheet from his lower body to know that he was naked. Beside him, Candy's too-thin frame stretched across the length of the bed. He too was naked, but unlike Jeff whose memory was a blank, Candy was smiling in anticipation of continuing their earlier sexual adventures.

Jeff groaned. "Stop it, Candy. What did I say?"

Candy's satisfied grin faded, replaced by a confused pout. "When?" he asked.

"When I got here yesterday," Jeff shouted. "What did I tell you?"

Candy's pout slipped into a frown. "You were talking weird, okay. You said that Phil Luxor made some statue and that it was alive, and it killed that old lady you picked up the other day and ate all her blood. Like I said, you were acting like you were drunk off your ass."

"What about the woman? Did I tell you anything about the succubus?"

"The what?" Candy raised himself on one elbow then slid his feet off the bed and sat up with his back to Jeff. "Were you with a woman before you came here?"

"Damn it, Candy. Did I say anything about a woman named Kissy Mantrap?"

With his back still to Jeff, Candy shook his head. "No. You were just babbling about how some big metal statue ate some woman. I'm telling you, Jeff. You were freaking me out." Candy turned his head and smiled. "But I'll forgive you if you give me a kiss."

Candy puckered slightly and leaned forward quickly, catching Jeff by surprise. Before he could pull away, Candy pressed his lips against Jeff's. At the touch, the taste of Candy's lips burned through Jeff's mouth, down his parched throat and into his stomach. He could taste the blood and tissue beneath the thin top layers of flesh that covered Candy's thin lips.

Jeff closed his eyes and allowed his mouth to slip open.

But then the hot pressure of Candy's mouth was gone.

Jeff's eyes shot open in time to see Candy being yanked off the bed and onto the floor. For a split-second, Candy's face was caught in a clownish expression of bug eyes and an o-ringed mouth. Then the face, with the rest of the body, disappeared off the side of the bed.

Jeff started to move toward his friend but two distinct sounds coming from the floor stopped him. The first was Candy's scream, a high-pitched feminine wail, which quickly devolved into a weak gurgling whimper. The second sound was more sublime, but infinitely more disturbing. It was the sound of paper being ripped from a spiral-ring notebook, an innocuous sound Jeff had heard thousands of times when he was in school. But there were no notebooks stashed beneath Candy's bed to be ripped, no secret diaries to provide convenient fodder for shredding.

There was only Candy and the thing that yanked him off the bed.

Jeff froze, not daring to lean over and watch his most recent lover's flesh being ripped from his body. As Candy screamed Jeff pictured Stella's corpse on the linoleum floor with her skin neatly flayed in ribbon-like strips. He knew what was being done to Candy.

Jeff froze.

And waited.

The ripping sound lasted much longer than the screaming. When it stopped Jeff breathed in deeply the scent of cigarettes and stale perfume. "Kissy," he whispered.

Beneath the bed came a shuffling. "Still haven't found my pretty face," her disembodied voice said from beneath the mattress.

Jeff stiffened at the sound.

"Once again we find our true nature's taking over. You fuck, and I feed," Kissy said. "And Metamorpho has been very thorough with your boyfriend, Jeff. Do you want to see?"

"No," Jeff said, even as his body was already inching toward the side of the bed.

"Oh come on, Jeff. You know you want to take just a

little peeky-weeky before I'm finished."

Jeff leaned across the bed and looked over the side.

The floor was bare.

"What?" This didn't make sense. Candy's body should have been sprawled out beneath him gutted like a fish. But there was nothing there. No body, no torn flesh. No blood.

Candy was gone.

But he wasn't.

Jeff snapped himself back into his seated position and looked down at his lower body. The mauve colored blanket was torn off the bed. Draped over his waist and legs in its place was an odd-shaped translucent sheet that reeked of sweat and blood. Jeff's face contorted into an oddly similar version of Candy's bug-eyed look when he saw a pair of hollow arms trailing from the sides of the sheet.

"Oh shit," Jeff wailed when he saw what had become of Candy. Somewhere from beneath the bed came the sound of Kissy's laughter.

Jeff screamed.

Then he shut his eyes.

Then screamed again.

And woke up.

TWENTY-FOUR

He was in his own room, still dressed in the same jeans and t-shirt he wore from when he went to Phil Luxor's apartment.

Jeff greedily inhaled the familiar aroma of his efficiency apartment, mildew and just a hint of the bug spray he had used the day before. He breathed in deeper. Yes, there it was. The smell of old feet that was permanently ground into the worn fabric of the carpet.

It was an unpleasant smell. Foul even.

But it wasn't the smell of warm blood and evil.

Hello my pretty one.

Jeff groaned, pushing himself out of bed. It was just a dream. Another total mind-fuck of a dream. It had been months since he'd had a nightmare that bad. But he'd had them before. He'd have them again. And as long as the memory of Kissy Mantrap liked to play hide and seek in his subconscious, the nightmares would come.

"No doubt about it," Jeff said, plucking a cigarette off the nightstand next to his bed. He lit the stick and ran his fingers across his scalp. He brushed back his greasy hair then sniffed his fingers and decided to forgo a shower. The clock on the nightstand burned the time in red numerals.

9:15 PM

Jeff allowed himself five minutes to finish his smoke before he started getting ready for work.

TWENTY-FIVE

Jeff was reaching for his timecard to check in when someone grabbed his arm, sharply pinching his left bicep. "Where the hell have you been?"

Yanking his arm free, Jeff spun around to face Mort Nevin, the nightshift supervisor and Jeff's boss. A small overweight man with a bad prostate, Mort was wiggling a pudgy finger at Jeff, his face skewed in a tight-lipped frown that turned the scalp beneath his thinning white hair a light shade of puce. "I don't know what the hell you did at your last job, but you sure-as-shit aren't going to get away with just taking off and not getting someone to cover your shifts."

"What are you talking about?" Jeff said, pushing himself past Mort. "I got off at five this morning."

Mort laughed and pulled Jeff's time card off the wall. "What kind of idiot do you take me for, French?" Mort shoved the cardboard slip in Jeff's face. "Read it. You haven't been here in three days."

Jeff snatched the card out of Mort's hand. He scanned the column that marked the time he started work with a black dot. There were no dots for the last three days. "This is bullshit," Jeff said, slamming the card back into its slot on the wall. "I worked my shift, and afterwards I went over to Phil's house."

At the mention of Phil's name, the frown on Mort's face deepened sending new traces of puce across his forehead. "Phil Luxor," he said. "That bastard hasn't been here either."

"Phil hasn't been to work?"

Nevin shook his head. "Nope. He hasn't been here either. Now I don't know what kind of games you and Luxor are playing, but your little vacation left us up to our asses in stiffs. The graveyard shift has had twenty-seven pick-ups in the last 72 hours. Twenty-seven pickups and no fucking drivers!" Mort tossed his hands in his air and stormed past Jeff toward the holding room where over half of the last three days pickups were still being stored. "It doesn't matter," he called over his shoulder. "I hired a new crew, so you and Luxor don't work here anymore. Clean your shit out of your locker and get the hell out of here."

"Wait a second," Jeff yelled as his boss flung open the swinging metal doors of the holding room. Jeff hurried down the hall after him. "I can prove I was here yesterday," Jeff said as he pushed open the heavy doors. "Ask Candy. He saw me and Phil leaving."

"Candy?" Nevin asked. He handed a young orderly a clipboard then turned his attention to Jeff. "You mean Harry Kane, don't you?"

"Yeah," Jeff shot back. "Harry Kane. He'll tell you."

The orderly and Mort exchanged a quick glance. "Listen," Mort said, his voice low and measured. "I don't know what kind of sick game you're playing with me, French. But if you know what's good for you, you'll turn around and get the fuck out of here."

"No. I can't afford to lose this job, and I'm not going to because there's some mistake on my punch card. Now I was here yesterday, and Candy will verify that."

Mort stood still, his body clenched to the point of quivering. "He will, will he?" Mort shouted. "Let's just see about that." Without explanation, Mort pushed past the orderly and headed to the long wall of metal drawers that housed the stiffs. Plucking a set of keys out of his pocket, Mort went up to the drawer number 45. "You want to se if Candy will vouch for you. Well, let's ask him."

As Mort inserted the key into the drawer, a cold understanding hit Jeff like a tire iron. It slammed into his head, his shoulders and chest; his legs buckled and the hot taste of vomit filled his mouth.

"Candy was pickup number 4, two nights ago," Mort said, yanking the drawer open. Jeff looked at the drawer, but there was no body stretched out on the cold, metal table. What sat there was a long metal basin with a white sheet draped over its side. "Whoever murdered Candy ripped him apart. Took his insides, his bones, everything. Shit," Mort said, his voice softening. "What we could find of him, we had to scrape into this bucket." Mort paused then shot Jeff a steely glance. "See for yourself."

Mort yanked the sheet off the basin revealing the hollowed-out skin that was all that remained of Harry "Candy" Kane.

TWENTY-SIX

The pounding caused Phil to jerk himself out of a dreamless sleep. He waited, not sure if the sound was real or a mild hallucination brought on from exhaustion. He listened through the silence as his eyes adjusted to the darkness around him. The pounding came again. This time more forceful, more urgent.

Phil forced his tired body off the couch and headed for the front door.

"Alright, I'm coming," he yelled. He easily navigated the dark passageways from the living room to the front door. For the past three days he had been holed up in his studio, surviving on strong coffee and bong hits. As he came to the door he glanced at his watch. It was almost ten, but Phil wasn't certain if that was AM or PM.

Phil undid the three locks on his front door and yanked it open. "Jeff," Phil said casually. "I thought it might be you." Phil stepped to the side and motioned for Jeff to come in.

"What have you done?" Jeff said as he brushed past Phil into the apartment. "What the fuck have you done?"

Phil ignored Jeff's outburst and calmly closed and rebolted the door. "What are you talking about, Jeff? I haven't done anything."

As Phil turned from the door, Jeff lunged forward and slammed his palms into Phil's chest, sending the artist into the wall. "Don't you lie to me!" Jeff grabbed a fistful of Phil's shirt then jammed his forearm beneath Phil's chin and started pushing. "You brought her back, didn't you?

You and that fucking machine in the gallery!"

Phil struggled against the pressure of Jeff's forearm, but the former porn star was too strong and fueled by too much adrenalin for Phil to wiggle himself free. Staring into the wide, blood shot eyes of his former partner, Phil Luxor felt his throat about to be crushed and realized he was going to die.

Then the pressure disappeared and Phil dropped to his knees.

Jeff took two steps back and collapsed ass first onto the floor. "You brought Kissy back, Phil. I killed her and you brought her back. And now she's killing again. Her and Metamorpho." Burying his face in his hands, Jeff began to weep.

Clutching his bruised neck, Phil swallowed a painful mouth of air as he shifted his weight from his knees onto his own rear end. "Calm down," Phil managed to choke out. "Just calm down."

His face still cupped in his hands, Jeff appeared not to have heard him.

Phil took three more deep breaths. Already the pain in his throat was subsiding. "What are you talking about? How can she be back? You said you shot her head off."

Slowly. Jeff took his hands from his tear-stained face and glared at Phil. "It's not her body," Jeff said. "It's her spirit. Her soul. Whatever the fuck it is that she has. She's gotten inside of Metamorpho, and she's using it to kill."

Phil rolled his eyes and groaned. "Come on, Jeff. I know we're caught up in some pretty weird shit, but Metamorpho is not killing anybody."

"He is," Jeff said. "I saw him. He killed Stella. You know, the lady you stole the hairpin from. Metamorpho shoved his arms right through her back. Then he went over to Candy's place and ripped his skin off his body."

"Candy," Phil said. "Harry Kane from the morgue?"

Jeff nodded. "Yeah. Metamorpho killed him two days

ago. I was there. Ripped him out of his bed and ate him. He didn't leave anything but his head and his skin."

Phil jumped to his feet. "Bullshit! Metamorpho is a fucking statue made out of chicken wire and metal pipe. He is not alive, and he is not possessed by the spirit of some succubus. That shit does not happen!"

"Yes it does," Jeff said sadly. "It happened, and it's your fault. You put all those things that held bits of people's souls into him. And that made him become, Phil. That made him become alive. You did that, Phil. You made him, and you made him hungry." Slowly, Jeff pushed himself off the floor and started down the hall toward Phil's studio.

"Come into the living room," Phil pleaded as he followed Jeff through the hall maze. "You look like you could use a beer and something to eat."

Jeff shook his head and continued toward the studio.

"What are you going to do?" Phil asked when the pair came upon the black door. Jeff's answer came without hesitation.

"Kill it." Stopping in front of the door, Jeff slipped his right hand into his leather jacket and removed the gun that had blown off Kissy Mantrap's head a year earlier. He half-turned and offered Phil a weak smile. "I've done it before."

Phil reached out to stop Jeff, but the younger man was too quick. Before Phil could get a hold of his coat, Jeff slammed shoulder first into the studio door and stumbled inside. The lights were off making it difficult for Jeff to see any more of his target than a large, shadowy outline. What was clear was the soft whir of Metamorpho's motor and the sound of a paintbrush scraping against the rough texture of the wall. The two sounds melted together perfectly into an inviting whisper.

Hello my pretty one.

A feeling of perfect calmness came upon Jeff as he aimed the gun at the base of the metal skeleton where he remembered the motor to be. He knew in all likelihood that his own death was just moments away; the spirit of the succubus would awaken Metamorpho and send the statue to rip him apart. It would hurt like hell, too, but that was a small price to pay for finally being free of Kissy Mantrap.

"Eat this," Jeff said as he pulled the trigger.

In the small, square studio, the gunshot exploded with the sound of a barely muffled cannon. Phil screamed as a streak of hot light erupted from the barrel, illuminating Jeff's face for a split-second in a field of white electricity. Hidden beneath the sound of the gun's discharge was the high-pitched shriek of metal hitting metal.

Jeff took aim again, but before he could fire, Phil switched on the lights.

"Stop it!" he shouted, but Jeff didn't waver. With a clear shot now, he adjusted his aim and fired a second round into the motor at the base of Metamorpho's skeleton. This bullet struck true, blasting the mechanism into a dozen pieces. Metamorpho's skeleton hitched to the left then quickly dropped its right arm parallel with the floor splattering droplets of red paint against the canvas on the wall. The pattern reminded Jeff of the goop on the wall of Henry Wallace's kitchen.

"No!" Phil wailed, rushing to the now still statue. He glanced about at the ruined canvas then down at the twisted gizmos on the floor. "Damn you!" Phil wheeled around. "Goddamn it, Jeff. What the fuck are you doing?"

"Putting a stop to this," Jeff said blankly, the gun aimed at a spot directly behind Phil's head. "Now get out of the way. I have four bullets left."

"And then what?"

"Then Kissy will have nowhere to go and this will all be over. Now please, Phil. Get out of the way."

"It's already over," Phil said, moving to his left so he was no longer in the line of fire. "Look at Kissy's painting. I fixed it. She's no longer a succubus."

"You fixed it?" Jeff laughed slightly but did lower the gun. "How the hell did you fix it?"

Phil hurried to the tarp that covered the work-in-progress. "I found a copy of that movie you were in, *Hard Attack*. I saw the girl," Phil said, yanking the tarp from the painting. "I saw what she looked like and painted her over the succubus."

The tarp was flung to the floor and the face of Kissy Mantrap in all her cold, sculpted beauty gazed down at Jeff from the canvas.

For a moment, the stunned expression on Jeff's face bordered on the comical, but Phil didn't dare laugh. Especially since Jeff still had the Smith and Wesson. But then Jeff's entire body went rigid as if he had suddenly been hit in the head with a two by four. His eyes flew open wide and his arms shot out to his sides. The gun slipped out of his hand and smacked the wood floor with a loud thud, but Jeff didn't appear to notice. He took two staggering steps toward the canvas as Phil backed away from the painting. "It's her," Jeff said, half-whispering. "You really found her." He stared at the painting, shaking his head in disbelief.

Phil slid behind Jeff and picked up the gun. "Yeah," he said. "I found her."

With his back turned to Phil, Jeff continued shaking his head. "You found her pretty face," he whispered. "You found her pretty face."

Jeff turned around and Phil nearly shot him.

Jeff's piercing blue eyes, the eyes that melted the heart of Candy Kane, had turned jet cold and lifeless like polished, black stones. If Phil had been closer, he would have seen twin mirrors of his terrified face reflected back at him.

"You found her pretty face."

Shaking, Phil raised the gun and aimed it at Jeff's chest. "What are you?"

The question hung in the air a moment before Jeff answered. "I don't know," he said, taking an awkward step forward. "I don't know."

Phil told himself not to shoot; he forced himself to remain calm, even though his friend was staring at him with the black dead eyes of a succubus.

And he would have been able to remain calm if Metamorpho didn't rip itself free of the wire and pulley system that had controlled its movements.

Phil screamed, and though he was staring at the headless, metal skeleton ripping itself free of the mechanism that housed it, Phil fired three shots directly into Jeff's chest. Before he could fire a fourth time, Metamorpho freed himself and slapped the gun out of Phil's hand. Phil tried to turn and run, but the metal arms of his creation wrapped themselves around his chest in a bear hug and turned him so he faced the canvas.

The force of the three bullets that struck Jeff's chest sent him staggering backward toward the portrait of Kissy Mantrap. He slammed up against it, his face upturned toward the ceiling and his arms outstretched as if he was being crucified. For a second, Phil thought he was going to call upon God to deliver him from evil, then Jeff's head slumped forward. His eyes were no longer black; they were crystal blue and glazed over with the look of a man who had a bird's eye view of hell. Jeff's entire body quivered and started to fall forward.

But it never hit the floor.

Instead, it said fuck you to every known law of physics by snapping back as if tethered to an elastic band with enough force to dislodge the painting, but instead of falling, the portrait of Kissy Mantrap started to vibrate. As Jeff's body flailed against the canvas, the image of Kissy Mantrap began to expand inside. She pushed herself forward until her face and torso pressed against the canvas, her perfect nose and cheeks flattening as if she was smooshing her face against a window. In any other circumstance, the image would have been comical to Phil. But watching a figure from one of his portraits trying to escape the painting while another piece of his artistic handiwork trapped him in a bear hug was more than enough to send the former ambulance driver barreling down the road to insanity. After about half a minute's struggle, Kissy was able to push her arms free of the canvas and, dripping of warm, flesh-tone paint, wrap themselves around Jeff's chest. She pulled the former porn star tight against the wall and squeezed.

And with Metamorpho's fingers digging into the flesh around his mouth, Phil found a way to scream. It was the kind of excruciating scream that would have shattered a champagne glass if one had been handy. But there wasn't any glass in Phil's studio, not even an old beer bottle lying around. So nothing shattered when Phil screamed.

Except for Jeff.

But he didn't really shatter; that would have been much cleaner resulting in just a bunch of little pieces of Jeff strewn about the floor like a broken windowpane. Instead, Jeff exploded. One second he was standing there getting a hug from Kissy Mantrap, and the next second he was a cloud of human shrapnel flying through the air. Tiny shards of Jeff's bones slapped Phil's face, ripping dozens of razor sharp cuts into his flesh, his own blood mixing with the rust-colored mist that blanketed the studio. Phil's eyes and throat pinched shut, but his nostrils remained open allowing him to breath in the secret smell of Jeff French's internal organs. Like burnt bratwurst, Phil thought. A hard roll and a side order of fries and we got ourselves a picnic.

Phil wanted to laugh, needed to laugh, but he was choking on the taste of what he thought was Jeff's spleen and couldn't find a way to laugh. But that part of his brain that was heading down that highway to insanity had set the cruise control at ninety and found the whole thing hilarious. That part of his brain was busting a gut.

But the part of Phil's brain that appreciated the depth of the shit he was in stayed silent. It pushed away the taste of Jeff's innards and the urge to vomit and forced Phil to open his eyes. Through the blood-red haze, Phil watched as Kissy Mantrap stepped out of the painting and onto a puddle of guts and tissue. She glanced around the room, ignoring both Phil and what was left of Jeff. She sniffed in the air once, then forming a tight O with her mouth, she inhaled. Immediately, the bits of flesh and blood that drifted like dust in the air were sucked into the cavity of her mouth.

This time Phil did laugh. To hell with sanity. Kissy Mantrap was inhaling the cloud of Jeff's blood the way Superman used to suck up the mustard gas that Lois Lane always found herself ankle deep in on that old TV show. But only Kissy wasn't doing the Hoover trick for truth, justice, and the American way. She was feeding and . . .

Phil's laughter melted into a sob.

Kissy was feeding and becoming . . .

Alive.

Phil screamed, and to his surprise, felt himself falling forward. He hit the ground and rolled over onto his side. Metamorpho was dragging its metal frame toward Kissy, waving its arms amidst the cloud of Jeff's flesh and blood trying to absorb as much as possible before Kissy engulfed it all. For a second, neither creature noticed Phil.

Phil scrambled to his feet and bolted for the door. He managed to round the corner and turn right into the hall before he heard Kissy tell Metamorpho to bring him back. Phil didn't hesitate. He ran past the cubicle that was the living room and through his den where he kept his television and stereo. Behind him the sound of Metamorpho crashing through the makeshift plywood walls echoed throughout the apartment.

Only a few steps ahead of the metallic skeleton, Phil

rushed into the gallery, the most direct way out of his apartment. He meant to exit through the door partially hidden by one of his larger portraits but stopped when he saw the transformation that had come over his paintings. The Luxor-like faces that filled his many portraits were all contorted in masks of agonizing pain and suffering. Their mouths were twisted into primal screams as the painted flesh dripped from their faces onto the floor below.

Phil stumbled toward the portrait of Gary Kenny. The man's face was almost completely melted away exposing his skull. Kenny's left eyeball hung from a loose strand of nerve, as his lower jaw snapped open in a silent scream. "No," Phil wailed as he watched Kenny's eyeball snap from the thread that held it and fall to the floor. Inside the painting, Kenny made a halting step forward.

Oh Christ, Phil thought. He's trying to escape.

Phil spun around to face the paintings of Lycan to discover that the mythic figure was no longer trapped within the canvas. Half of Lycan's fully transformed body writhed in the air, his enormous wolf head whipping back and forth. With each movement, Lycan inched forward.

Look at your art, Kissy's voice thundered in his head. *They're all becoming something new. Something wonderful.*

Lycan was nearly free, his jaws snapping within arms length of Phil when the artist felt himself being lifted off the ground. Metamorpho had crept into the room and wrapped its metal arms once again about Phil's chest.

Phil didn't struggle, he didn't scream as Metamorpho carried him through the shattered walls of his apartment back to the studio. When they arrived, Kissy was still enraptured in her feeding frenzy. Her mouth open and head tilted back, the reddish air poured into her mouth like liquid. As the cloud grew less thick, Metamorpho's grip on Phil tightened until the artist thought he would be crushed.

When he thought he heard the howl of a werewolf reverberate through his apartment, Phil hoped that

Metamorpho would keep on squeezing. But it didn't.

When the last of the blood cloud was sucked down her throat, Kissy closed her mouth and trained her black-eyed gaze on Phil. For a second, Phil could see his reflection in her eyes, then Kissy blinked, and when her eyelids flipped back open, the eyes that stared back at Phil were a vibrant green. Kissy smiled, and Phil thought she was the most beautiful woman he'd ever seen.

"You found my pretty face," Kissy said, absently wiping a few drops of blood from her mouth with the back of her hand. She glanced at the floor and gently pushed away some of Jeff's remains with the tip of her right foot. "I knew you would."

"You did?" Phil was surprised that he could speak.

Kissy nodded. "Certainly. You're a special man, Phil Luxor, with more than one useful talent. But you are also arrogant, and that, my artistic friend, is what led me to you." Kissy laughed and tossed her auburn hair back over her shoulders. "Did you really think the dead were contacting you? Begging you to help them metamorphosize?" Kissy stepped over what remained of Jeff's left arm and shoulder. Phil flinched when Kissy brought her arm out, but when her fingers caressed his cheek, Phil felt an undeniable stirring in his groin. "It's been me the whole time, Phil. I'm the one who has been calling you. Telling you to steal those bits of soul for our metal friend there." Kissy's hand slipped from Phil's cheek.

Instinctively, Phil strained his head forward toward her touch. More than anything, he wanted to feel her fingers against his skin.

But Kissy denied him what would have been his last pleasure. She took two steps back, just beyond arm's reach.

The disappointment was overwhelming. "Jeff killed you," Phil managed to say.

Kissy didn't argue. "Some of me, yes. But not all of me," Kissy replied. "He didn't kill my eyes."

"Your eyes?"

Kissy nodded. "The eyes hold our hunger, who we are, who we are meant to be. They truly are the windows to the soul, Phil. As an artist, you should know that." Kissy took another step away from Phil which made the stirring in his groin even more pronounced. "When your friend told you about our encounter, he neglected to mention one thing. Before he escaped, I ripped his eyes from their sockets and replaced them with mine."

Jeff's eyes. The eyes Phil thought were so pale and perfect. "Why? I don't understand."

"So I could see. Isn't that obvious?" Phil's blank look told Kissy that nothing was obvious. Kissy frowned. "Your friend took away my pretty face," she said, running her thin fingers against her cheek and through her hair. "And I wanted it back. You see, I could have come back any time, but I needed something to come back through." Kissy turned to the blank canvas that hung limply from the wall. "That's why you were needed. Your arrogance and curiosity provided that portrait for me." Kissy spun around to face Phil. "But before I could come through, I had to make sure that you painted the right face. The face I wanted. That's why I needed your friend. He carried my eyes. And you did all the rest."

"But the people," Phil began. "Jeff said you possessed Metamorpho and ate people. He said you ate Harry Kane."

"Oh no. You can't blame me for Metamorpho. You're the one who created him. You're the one who gave him life." Kissy laughed "So you're responsible for his actions. That's how creation works. But as for Jeff, he carried much more than my eyes," Kissy said, moving toward Phil. "He carried my hunger as well. Like you, like your statue, I am a living thing. I have a soul. And because of that I have to feed." Kissy glanced down and casually brushed her foot against what was left of Jeff's spine. "Jeff was my food long before you ever met him. But enough talking. We have much to do."

Phil screamed as Kissy's pretty face melted into the twisted mask of the succubus. "It is time to become, artist."

TWENTY-SEVEN

Officer Lance Jacobs swallowed hard as he surveyed the bloody mess that was Phil Luxor's studio, and wondered how long he had to go until retirement. Thankfully, he didn't have to go in the room. That was a job for forensics.

"What do you think happened, Lance?"

Jacobs looked at his young partner, an ashen face rookie named Bill Steever. "Beats the hell out of me. I just know it was bad."

Steever nodded. "It looks like the guy got ripped apart."

"Two guys," Jacobs said blankly.

"Huh?"

Jacobs pointed to a mound of bones in the corner of the studio. "Look at the bones. I don't know a hip bone from the leg bone, but I sure as hell know what a hand looks like, and there's two hands in that pile."

Steever allowed himself a glance at the bones. "Yeah," he said. "So?"

"So look at that pile of shit beneath that painting."

"Oh man," Steever hissed as he recognized what his partner was pointing at. Amidst a pile of fresh entrails and ripped flesh, a left hand attached to the bottom half of a severed arm lay flattened on the floor.

"Yeah," Jacobs said. "Another hand. Another corpse."

Steever took his cap from his head and wiped the back of his hand across his mouth. He closed his eyes and took a deep breath. He was one bad smell away from blowing chunks, and he didn't want to do it in front of Jacobs.

"What the hell happened here?" he asked, his eyes still screwed tight.

"Something bad," was Jacob's reply. "Something really fucking bad."

TWENTY-EIGHT

The cruise control of the Mustang convertible was set at seventy-five. With the top rolled down, the wind whipped her auburn hair in wild swirls about her face as she headed westward to the coast. Hidden behind a pair of mirrored sunglasses, her black eyes burned with hunger. She would need to feed soon.

"We're going to stop in the next town," she said, not taking her eyes from the road.

Phil Luxor's head lolled to the side.

"Do you understand what I said?"

Phil's lips parted.

It hurts.

Kissy turned to face him. She smiled and brought her hand up to caress his cheek. The expression on Phil's face remained unchanged as she stroked it. It was the same expression he wore when she ripped his head from his shoulders, a fusion of terror and wonder. It was the expression the former artist would wear for eternity.

Or at least until the metal skeleton of Metamorpho could no longer support his head. Even with the fragments of souls Phil had collected, Metamorpho was nothing more than a twisted piece of metal with an insatiable hunger. He had yet to become fully alive. To do that, he needed to become one with his creator. "The ultimate fusion of art and artist," Kissy had told Phil as she ripped his still beating heart from his chest and jammed it into Metamorpho's metal frame. "You'll be famous, Phil. Isn't that what you've always wanted?" she taunted as she eviscerated him. "To be a star in the firmament of heaven?"

But Phil no longer wanted anything so grand. As Kissy ripped open his insides, Phil only wished for death, but like fame, even that was denied him. Just as his heart and lungs were now part of Metamorpho, so too was Phil's soul, his hunger. He was undead, sharing the metal hell of his creation with the souls he had collected. He had become...

Damned.

Kissy looked over her handiwork, pleased at the way she was able to stretch Phil's skin around Metamorpho's frame. It was a perfect fit, except for a portion of the lower torso where about twenty yards of Phil's intestines were twisted through chicken wire. That part of Phil's new body still needed some work.

But, after all, Phil was a work in progress.

It hurts.

Phil's head swiveled on the pipe that was pounded through the top of his skull and soldered to Metamorpho's chest cavity. Kissy noticed the looseness of the fit and made a mental note to insert a plate between the pipe and what was left of Phil's skull. A few well-placed screws would do the trick, but that could wait. For now she would feed.

"I'll fix you tomorrow," Kissy promised.

A single tear formed in Phil's eye.

It hurts.

"Yes." Kissy replied, turning her attention back to the road. She felt no pity for her creation, no sympathy for the brutal pain he was forced to endure. She only felt the eager hunger that consumed her soul.

"It's supposed to hurt, Phil. But think of it as suffering for your art."

Printed in the United States
PP569200002B/2